Shooting Hollywood

MELODIE JOHNSON HOWE

Shooting Hollywood

The Diana Poole Stories

by Melodie Johnson Howe

Crippen & Landru Publishers
Norfolk, Virginia
2011

Cover by Gail Cross

Crippen & Landru logo by Eric D. Greene

ISBN (signed, limited clothbound edition): 978-1-932009-99-6
ISBN (trade softcover edition): 978-1-936363-00-1

FIRST EDITION

10 9 8 7 6 5 4 3 2 1

Printed in the United States of America on recycled acid-free paper

Crippen & Landru Publishers
P. O. Box 9315
Norfolk, VA 23505
USA

www.crippenlandru.com
info@crippenlandru.com

FOR JANET HUTCHINGS

CONTENTS

INTRODUCTION

Acting, *The Pat Hobby Stories* by F. Scott Fitzgerald, and my love of the mystery genre are the major influences in creating these stories.

When I was twenty-one I was put under contract to Universal Studios. I was one of the last starlets; one of the last contract players. The times were changing and soon the entire studio system would be a free-for-all of lawyers, accountants, and independent production companies. This would be followed by the onslaught of conglomerates funded by such products as bottled water, soda, vodka, and computers, which gobbled up what was left of the great old studios. This is the new Hollywood that the actress Diana Poole knows.

The business of show business was always ugly and brutal. Today it is no different. As William Faulkner said, "Hollywood is a place where a man can get stabbed in the back while climbing a ladder." Or as Marilyn Monroe put it so beautifully, "Hollywood's a place where they'll pay you a thousand dollars for a kiss, and fifty cents for your soul ..."

Also at twenty-one I married Bones Howe, who had three children. (Bones and I are still married and the 'children' are thriving adults.) If marriage, instant motherhood, and a fledgling career in the movies, wasn't enough, I really wanted to be a writer. When I wasn't acting, I would go to the UCLA Extension at night and take writing courses in fiction. It was there I began to learn the craft of the short story. I will never forget the first critique of my work from a male student who said, "How can you write with a body like that?" I retorted, "I don't write with my body."

So my love/hate relationship with Hollywood and my "movie star" looks were set, and now they fuel Diana Poole's character along with hope and cynicism – an odd combination for sure, but not if you're an actor. Or for that matter, a writer.

When I first read *The Pat Hobby Stories* I knew that I too wanted to write stories about Hollywood. Fitzgerald captured the desperation of an over-the- hill and out of work screenwriter who would do anything to get back on the studio lot to "take" a meeting. Any meeting. The demeaning extremes Pat Hobby was willing to go to are hilarious and sad.

Of course *The Pat Hobby Stories* were not driven by crime unless it's the crime of the ego, and I wanted to keep both feet firmly planted in the genre I loved.

Throughout the sixties and the seventies I acted, raised our children, and triedto hone the craft of writing. It wasn't until I was up for a role (I no longer remember what it was) when I walked into a room filled with blondes – all of us eerily similar, all vying for the same part – that I said to myself, "This is it. It's time to stop. You want to be a writer, write." I turned around and walked out and have never been in front of a camera again.

Setting myself up in an empty bedroom in our home, I began to write. Not an easy task for an actress who was always surrounded by wardrobe and make-up people, the other actors, the crew, the director, and the security of a script. But I somehow made the transition from all of that attention to the isolating loneliness of being a writer.

A few years later I was attending the Edgar Award Ceremony. My book, *The Mother Shadow*, had been nominated for Best First Novel. It was there that Marilyn Wallace came up to me and asked if I would like to write a short story for a *Sisters in Crime 4* anthology.

I went back to Los Angeles, the dusty palm trees, the Technicolor sunsets created by the smog, and thought about acting, Pat Hobby, and crime. I wrote a short story titled, "Dirty Blonde." And as they say in Hollywood a star was born. Well, at least an actress trying to get work while being thwarted by betrayal and murder, Diana Poole.

Melodie Johnson Howe
Santa Barbara, California

This story came about because a man who managed the Mysterious Bookstore many years ago in Los Angeles was robbed of a rare first edition (I believe it was a Raymond Chandler novel), and described the culprit to the police as being a dirty blonde. This robbery has nothing to do with the subject of the short story, but those two words "dirty blonde" were a catalyst for it.

DIRTY BLONDE

I had rejected Gordon Keith, sexually that is, many times when I was a young and up-and-coming actress. What made it awkward was that Gordon knew he was one of just a few men I had rejected. In Hollywood, where everyone strives for some sort of difference, this made him fairly unique. Now, ten years later, as I sat across from him in his office, I knew it was a distinction he would still rather have done without.

"You look great," he said, leaning intimately across his desk as if we were at a table for two in some dark corner of a restaurant. His fleshy hands came to rest on the television script.

"Thank you," I said.

"So, Diana, you want to get back into acting." His dark eyes drifted over my body, then settled on my face.

"I need the money and it's all I know how to do."

"Colin never did know how to handle his money."

He was right. Colin Hudson, my husband, believed you wrote hard, spent hard, and lived well.

"I'm going to miss the son-of-a-bitch," he said. I smiled. Most writers in Hollywood are constantly referred to that way. But in Colin's case it was spoken with admiration. He was one of the few writers who knew how to wheel-and-deal for himself. It was believed he could have run a studio if he hadn't been so creative. Thinking about him brought back that wrenching pain of emptiness I'd been waking up to every morning since his death eight months before.

Gordon spread open his hands, peered down at the script, then slowly back at me.

"What do you think of the part? You don't mind playing a mother?"

"I'm old enough to play the mother of a twenty-year-old."

"Always so direct, so honest." This wasn't spoken with admiration.

"Who do I read with? You? The director?" I asked.

"You don't have to read for me."

"I haven't acted in ten years."

"It's not that big a role. Besides, the deal's done."

"What do you mean?"

"I called your agent. We'll pay what he asked. This is just a courtesy meeting. Just to see you."

"Thanks, Gordon."

He leaned back in his chair. "You look like you still have great tits."

I said nothing. What was there to say? We stared at one another.

"You know we're going to have to play 'em down. America isn't ready for mothers with great tits."

He smiled. I smiled.

"One thing," he leaned forward spreading his hands flat on the script.

"Yes?"

"A favor."

There had to be one. But I didn't think it was going to be sexual. I was now in my forties and Gordon liked them young.

"Don't worry, I'm not going to ask you to go to bed with me."

"I wasn't worried, Gordon."

Again we smiled.

"It's the actress Wynn Larkin. She's going to play your daughter. I want you to look after her."

"In what way?"

"It's her first starring role. She's scared as hell. You've been through it. You know what it's all about. Just talk to her. Try to help her."

"Sure."

"And then report back to me."

"Report?"

"Yeah. Tell me how she's doing."

"Won't you see how she's doing in dailies?"

"If she's nervous or afraid and I see it on film it's already too late."

"What about Howard Marsh?"

"He should've been a plumber instead of a director. You know it. I know it. He's going to get his shot. That's all he cares about. I didn't want him but he gets the show done on time. Hey, that's what it's all about in television. Time. That's why I don't want her staying out late. Seeing anybody. You let me know who she's seeing."

"There's a difference between looking out for someone and spying on them."

He stared down at his hands, lifted them from the script, contemplated it, then slowly raised his head and contemplated me. "You know Diana, you look great but you're middle-aged now. This town is filled with middle-aged actresses who have stayed in the business and are looking for work. They'd kill for this role. You left the business. I'm giving you a chance to get back in it. You can take that chance or not."

In Hollywood, like Nazi Germany, there are people in power who think they are better human beings than the rest of us. Gordon was one of them.

"Besides," he continued, "I think it might help you to fill the void a little bit. I think you'll like her. She reminds me of you when you were her age. Blonde, sexy. A great mouth. A dirty mouth. Not in the way she talks, in the way of possibilities. Do you know what I mean?"

"I think so." I stood.

"Just a minute." He pushed one of many buttons on his telephone. The door opened. Rose, his secretary, came in. She had been with

Gordon for as long as I could remember. Her momentary youth had turned to a brittle officiousness.

"Yes, Mr. Keith?"

"Get Mrs. Hudson a script."

She hurried out of the office.

"You can use my professional name, Gordon."

"I think of you as Colin's wife."

It was a put-down. But I had the role. I had to keep telling myself that. I had the role.

"Now you can think of me as Diana Poole."

"The Diana Poole I knew was a dirty blonde. That's a compliment. You know how I like dirty blondes, and you were the best."

"The best at what, Gordon?"

He didn't answer. He just grinned, knowingly. I wanted out of his office before I told him to take his role and shove it up his ass. The one thing success does for you in Hollywood is allow you to lie to yourself. Success makes you think you have principles. Right now I couldn't afford the luxury of self-deception.

Rose came back in with a script and handed it to me.

"Your appointment in wardrobe is in fifteen minutes, Mrs. Hudson," she announced.

"I made it for you," Gordon explained. "Save you the extra trip from driving into town from the beach."

"Say hello to Vivian for me."

He stared at me as if he'd forgotten his wife's name. "Oh, yeah, sure."

I walked out of the Executive Building. It was a hot August day and the sun pierced through the brown air with the sharpness and accuracy of a laser. I put on my sunglasses and walked across the street past the commissary, where my picture had once hung on the wall, and turned down a narrow tree-lined street. Being back on the studio lot was like coming back to the small town where you grew up. There is the illusion of sameness and yet everything has changed. The people look familiar but you really don't remember them and they don't remember you.

A black Mercedes with darkened windows pulled up beside me and stopped. The window on the passenger side slipped down and I heard a woman's voice.

"Hello, Diana."

It was Vivian, Gordon Keith's wife.

"How are you Vivian?" I asked peering into the car.

"May I talk to you for a moment?"

"I have to be in wardrobe."

"Just for a minute." She leaned over and opened the door. I got in.

"Close the door. I have the air conditioning on," she said.

I did. She pushed a button and my window slipped quietly up. I was surrounded by cool black leather and the smell of Chanel No. 5, a perfume I've always detested. Vivian turned toward me resting her arm on the steering wheel. She had on a short black leather skirt. Her legs were still great looking. The shape of an ex-dancer's legs always endure. But the years had not been kind to the rest of her. The hair was too blonde. In fact, I didn't remember her ever being blonde. Lines dug deep around her coral-painted lips giving her face a pinched look. The color of her once beautiful sharp green eyes had faded, but the diamonds on her ring finger, around her neck, and clasping her lobes shone brilliantly. The Mercedes purred.

"It's been a long time, Vivian," I said.

"Yes. I was very surprised last night when Gordon told me you were coming in to read for his movie. I take it if you're on your way to wardrobe you got the part."

"I think Gordon gave it to me for old times sake."

"Gordon doesn't give without a reason. You should've heard how he went on about you last night."

"Gordon always talks up the actors in his movies."

"He was only talking about you to me. His wife. My God, it was like nothing had changed. I felt like I did fifteen years ago when I was watching you two at a party. Watching him rest his hand on your waist. Watching you throw back your head and laugh. Watching you turn and walk away. Your blonde hair swaying in perfect unison with your hips.

I watched him follow you. And all the time I'm the wife sitting on the sofa talking about some fucking cooking class to some other dumb wife. And forty-five minutes later Gordon is casually standing in front of me, smiling down at me. And then you saunter in, look in the mirror, and smooth your hair."

"Vivian, I don't remember what you're talking about. Look, we're two middle-aged women who gave up our careers when we got married. I've lost my husband, a man I loved. And now I'm trying to put my life back together again by working at the only thing I know how to do. That's all."

I started to open the car door. She grabbed my wrist. Her grip was strong. She still had the strength of a dancer.

"Exactly. You've lost your husband and that makes you needy. That makes you vulnerable, right where Gordon wants you. He can offer you his strong shoulder to cry on. He can kiss your tears away."

"Let go of my wrist, Vivian."

Slowly she released my arm.

"Listen to me, I never went to bed with Gordon. I never wanted to. I never trusted him. This may come as a shock to you, but I never found your husband attractive."

"Did you trust all the men you went to bed with? Did you find them all attractive?"

I didn't answer her. I couldn't. When I was a young actress sex was my only power over the constant fear of rejection by those suited men, sitting behind their desks, picking one young actress over another for some bikini-clad role. Vivian and I should be two older, wiser women sitting in a Mercedes laughing at ourselves. But Vivian never could laugh.

"I'm late." I opened the car door.

"Diana, I swear to God, you come back into my husband's life and I'll kill you."

"For once in your life, Vivian, do something constructive for yourself. Divorce the bastard."

I got out of the car and walked up the sidewalk to wardrobe. She gunned the Mercedes. I could hear her backing down the narrow street at high speed.

As I entered the building I wondered if the imagined loss of someone you love was as deeply wounding as the actual loss of a loved one. Could the rage of jealousy be as strong and as everlasting as the reality of death?

I gave my name to a young woman who was sitting at a desk. She smoked a cigarette with a defiant theatrical jadedness. Only her youth kept her from being embarrassing. She located my name on a list, checked it, and told me to follow her.

"In here," she said without opening the dressing room door for me. She walked busily away. I went in.

She was blonde. She stood in front of a three-way mirror in her white lace bra and panties staring intently at her beautiful long-legged, high-breasted body.

"God, I'm so fat." She spoke to her reflection.

"Excuse me, I was told to come in here," I said backing out of the room.

"Aren't you Diana Poole?"

"Yes."

"It's the right room. I'm Wynn Larkin. I'm going to play your daughter."

"How do you do?" I put out my hand. She took it and gave it a limp shake. I sat down on a small gray sofa.

"God, I've put on so much weight." She twisted around and looked over her shoulder into the mirror so she could get a good view of her round, firm ass. "They say the camera puts ten pounds on you."

"Twelve," I corrected.

"God, I'm going to look like a house."

She turned and stood in front of me as if I were the mirror. She ran her hand across her flat belly. I could see her dark pubic hair through her gauzy white bikini. So she wasn't a natural blonde. I didn't think it would hold her back.

"Do you think I'm too fat?" she demanded.

"You know you're not fat. You know you look great standing there."

"So you don't like to bullshit." She sat down in a chair opposite me and crossed her long legs. "I do. It helps me when I'm nervous."

She didn't look fat. She didn't look nervous. I watched her dangle her black high-heeled shoe from the toes of her right foot.

"Gordon said you might help me with my lines."

"Be glad to."

"He said you live at the beach. So do I. He drove me in this morning. So I don't have a car. I wondered if you'd mind taking me home."

"Not at all."

"He just picked me up. My car isn't running."

"You don't have to explain."

"Okay, I'm having an affair with him. Everybody knows, even his wife." She smiled.

Gordon was right. She had the type of smile that suggested all kinds of sexual possibilities. But I would never have thought of it as dirty. But then I didn't think of sex as dirty. Gordon did. That's why I'm sure he loved to cheat on his wife. Sex with a wife wasn't naughty enough for him. Maybe that's why I never went to bed with Gordon. We didn't share the same view of sex. Wynn got up and stretched, then languidly reached for a white mini skirt the size of a tea cozy. She wiggled into it and pulled on a tight white T-shirt.

"I have to go to makeup. They want to change the color of my hair. Make it more golden or something. I kinda like my color. Gordon calls it dirty blonde." She giggled. It was a strange, spasmodic laugh connected to nothing funny.

"Can I meet you at your car?" she asked.

"Sure. I'm in the underground parking lot in the Executive Building."

"What kind is it?"

"Green Jag. It's unlocked. My air conditioner's not working so I left the windows down."

"I've always wanted a Jag," she said moving toward the door. "Oh," she stopped and looked at me. "I saw you talking to Mrs. Keith."

"Yes?"

"I recognized her car. What did she have to say?"

"It was just a conversation between two old friends," I lied.

"I thought she might have said something about me."

"No."

"Gordon tells her everything. Everything that he and I do with each other."

"Do you like that?"

For a moment her mouth looked soft, almost sweet. But it was only a moment. "She has a great car. I wouldn't mind having a Mercedes. See ya."

Wynn left me feeling I was being drawn into something. Something Gordon wanted.

The wardrobe mistress shuffled in wearing bedroom slippers and hung three dresses on the clothes rack.

"I'll be right back with your shoes," she said in a tired voice, and scuffed out of the room.

I got up and looked at the dresses. They were perfect if I were doing *Tobacco Road.*

An hour later I walked down the ramp into the underground garage. I removed my sunglasses, letting my eyes adjust from the bright sunlight to the cool darkness. My heels echoed the sound of a lone female as I made my way toward the car. And again I felt the sharp pain of loss.

I didn't see Wynn. I didn't see anybody until I approached the driver's side of the Jag. Gordon was sitting in the passenger seat.

"You always lurk in underground garages, Gordon?" I asked, sliding into the car. My skirt hiked up and I felt something warm on my thigh. Gordon didn't answer. I looked at him. His head flopped back against the head rest. His mouth sagged. One eye was open, the other closed as if he'd died in the middle of a leering wink. Blood trickled down from a hole in the side of his head. Slowly I became aware of bits and pieces of his hair and flesh on the burl wood dashboard. His hand rested casually on a gun. I looked down at my thigh. Blood was smeared across it.

"Oh, my God, oh, my God." Wynn stood next to the car quivering, repeating over and over. "Oh, my God, my God." Then she screamed and ran toward the ramp.

I stared straight ahead at the cement wall in front of me. Soon I heard footsteps and voices coming toward the car. But I was afraid they wouldn't be able to find me. It was getting dark in the garage. So dark.

"Colin," I murmured, opening my eyes. My mouth was dry. I was lying down trying to bring the recessed lighting into focus.

"I beg your pardon?"

The man's voice came from somewhere across a room.

"Colin."

"Who's Colin?" the voice asked.

I slowly sat up and swung my legs around. I was on the red leather sofa in Gordon's office. I stared at the smeared dry blood on my thigh and it all came back to me. I pulled my skirt down.

"Who is Colin?" he asked again.

Sitting behind Gordon's desk was a lean, unassumingly handsome man in a cheap suit. He was about my age. His intelligent blue eyes studied me.

"Colin is my husband."

"He was in the garage?"

"No, no. Colin's dead. Died of a heart attack. Who are you?"

"David Lang, L.A.P.D., Detective. Homicide."

"Yes, of course, the police. Homicide?"

"There's a dead body."

"How long have I been out?"

"About an hour. We had the studio doc check you."

He peered at Gordon's telephone with all the buttons and began pushing each one. Finally the door opened and Rose came in; her skin was as gray as her hair.

"Did he keep any booze in here?" he asked.

"In there." She pointed to a lacquered cabinet.

"That'll be all," he said.

"Mr. Howard March, the director, is outside. He wants to know if you're ... well, if you're ..."

"Yes?"

"Going to arrest Mrs. Hudson."

"Diana Poole," I said automatically. "Arrest?" That word didn't come out so easily.

She turned to me. "I'm sorry, but Mr. Marsh doesn't know whether he should recast or not. Your scenes shoot tomorrow. He's in a terrible snit."

Now we both looked at Detective Lang who was taking a glass and a bottle of brandy from the cabinet.

"Tell him to wait," he ordered.

Rose sighed and left the room.

He poured the glass full of brandy, handed it to me, then sat back down in Gordon's chair.

"I saw you, a long time ago, in a Burt Reynolds movie. Something about truckers," he said.

"*Highway Blues.*"

"I was on a date. Took her to a drive-in. I was going to score. You came on the screen. I'd never seen anyone so beautiful, so sexy."

Score? I hadn't heard that word in twenty years. Not since I was so beautiful. So sexy.

"Are you thinking of arresting me?"

"My date, I can't remember her name now, she was kind of cute and plump. But I kept looking at you. Now and then I'd sneak a look at her and suddenly she became just this plain, fat girl. Did you kill him?"

"No. Did you score?" I took another swig of brandy.

"No. Why don't you tell me what happened from the moment you arrived at the studio."

I told him everything that had occurred. But there were nuances I couldn't quite capture.

"Hard to think of you playing a mother to that blonde bimbo," he said.

"I don't like the word bimbo. I was called the equivalent of that when I was young and trying to make it. I'd like to wash the blood off my leg, if you don't mind."

"It's on your thigh."

"My thigh."

"I have this need for exactness. Drives people crazy, including my ex-wife. You can't wash the blood off your pantyhose. I assume you're wearing pantyhose. We may need them for evidence. I can get Sergeant Blake in here to help you. She's seen it all."

"I'd just like to throw some water on my face."

"Sure. Right in there." He leaned back in Gordon's chair, cocked his hand as if it were a gun – a gesture I could have done without – and pointed toward a door by the liquor cabinet.

The bathroom was done in black marble and tan wall paper. The toilet seat was up. I raised my skirt and looked down at the caked blood. I wasn't wearing anything under my pantyhose. I never did. What the hell, I'd had enough of Gordon Keith. I pulled off the pantyhose and wrapped them in a hand towel. The towel smelled of Chanel No. 5. It was strong. Vivian had been in this bathroom sometime during the day. I slipped my skirt back down. The silky lining felt cool against my buttocks and thighs, making me aware of my nakedness. I slipped on my shoes; they felt stiff on my bare feet. I thought of Wynn, with her long naked legs, dangling her black high-heeled shoe from her toes. I turned on the water, washed my hands, and dabbed at my face with a damp towel. I needed lipstick. I smoothed my hair and thought of Vivian remembering me looking into a mirror, smoothing my hair. A moment in the past which meant nothing to me, and yet meant so much to her.

Lang was just hanging up the phone when I walked out of the bathroom. I placed my little bundle in front of him.

"Here's your evidence."

He picked it up and smelled the towel. He did this as if he were judging the bouquet of a glass of wine.

"Not your perfume. Yours is more subtle, cleaner smelling."

"Chanel No. 5. Vivian Keith wears it. Have you talked to her?" I asked, sitting back down on the sofa.

"How did you know about this TV role?" he asked, purposely ignoring my question.

"Sam Marks is Colin's agent. Was Colin's agent. He's been a friend to both of us for years. He handles writers mostly. But when I told him I wanted to get back into acting he said he would help me out. He set up the appointment with Gordon Keith."

"Small role."

"I'm not exactly in demand."

"You went to bed with him. Doesn't that count for something?"

"Who told you that?"

"The bim... Wynn Larkin."

"Well, I didn't go to bed with him. But I'm the only one who seems to think I didn't."

"Probably doesn't matter. Just had a phone call. It seems the men way high up at this studio are talking to the people way high up downtown. And they, being such good detectives, think it's a case of suicide. Closed case. What do you think?"

"Was it his gun?"

"Yes."

"His fingerprints on the gun?"

"Hasn't been thoroughly checked yet, but unless you were so careless as to leave yours, I bet they're his."

"Why my car?"

"Good as place as any, I guess."

"Who do you think killed him?"

"I think Vivian Keith did it. Or Wynn Larkin did it. Or Diana Poole did it."

He turned and began pushing the buttons on the phone. Rose came in.

"Tell Marsh he doesn't have to get a new actress for the role." He looked at me. "Sergeant Blake will drive you home."

"I have a six o'clock makeup call in the morning," I told Rose. "I'm without a car."

"Mr. Marsh said that under the circumstances he'd have a car pick you up." She walked briskly out of the office.

"I'll be talking to you," Lang said, casually resting his hand on the towel wrapped around my pantyhose. "Too bad this is evidence. I'd like to keep it. Might be worth something one day. Famous producer's blood on actress's intimate apparel." He leaned back and laughed.

The phone rang. Its shrill scream knifed into my sleep. I awoke breathing hard, as if I'd been running. Reaching across the empty side of the bed I grabbed the receiver.

"Hello?" I blinked at the clock, it was three-thirty in the morning.

"You finally took him away from me." It was Vivian. She was either doped or drunk. "You took him away from me. You murderer! You bitch! You slut!"

I hung up on her. I lay back down and stared up at the ceiling. I could hear the ocean slapping against the sand. The telephone rang again. I leaned over and grabbed it.

"Look, Vivian, I didn't fuck your husband. I didn't kill your husband."

There was silence, then that strange disconnected giggle.

"It's Wynn, Diana."

"What do you want?"

"I can't sleep. I keep thinking about Gordon. And I try to study the script and I can't remember my lines."

"Marsh doesn't know how to move actors around for a whole page of dialogue. Don't worry about your lines."

"Gordon said you were great in bed. Gordon said there was nobody better, not even me."

I felt my body turn cold. I pulled the blankets up around me.

"I had to tell the detective that," she said. "I had to tell the truth. I'm going to look awful tomorrow. Big dark circles under my eyes."

"Do you have a boyfriend, Wynn?"

"What?"

"You heard me. Gordon thought you did."

She giggled. "Goodnight, Diana."

Again, I stared up at the ceiling. Everyone thought I had gone to bed with Gordon Keith. Even Gordon. I had the feeling that my life might be easier at this moment if I had gone to bed with him. I got up and stared out the window. The moon draped a silver glow over the water and the sand. I knew one thing. Gordon would never kill himself. He wasn't that thoughtful. So was it the wife? Or the girlfriend? I watched a man walk a large black poodle near the water's edge. Its pom-poms were silhouetted in the moonlight. Welcome back to Hollywood, Diana.

"Action!"

I moved from my mark, a strip of tape with my initials written on it, which had been stuck to the carpeting. I walked around the coffee table to the desk, hitting my next mark. The brilliant lights were warm on my face and arms. I had forgotten how comforting that warmth was. I could feel the makeup, a tight drying layer on my face. I opened the desk drawer, pretended to search through it, found the letter the prop man had put in there, took it out, opened it, pretended to read, brought my hand to my mouth – a corny gesture – and repeated my lines.

"Oh, my God, oh, my God." Then I screamed.

"Cut!" Marsh snapped.

I stopped screaming.

"Print," he commanded.

"Next set up. Clear the set! Clear the set!" the first assistant director yelled.

I made my way over the cables and around the lights.

"The hand gesture was a bit much, wasn't it?" Vivian wore dark glasses. "Oh, my God, Oh, my god," she imitated me.

I stared at her, but thought of Wynn standing in the garage by my car saying the exact same words. She had even screamed the way I had just screamed. The way it was written in the script. The trouble with clichéd writing is that it's usually true. Tired and unilluminating, but true. People did react that way.

"What are you doing here, Vivian?"

"Do you know they've already given Gordon's parking space away?"

Following me toward the sound stage door she said, "I have to talk to you."

We walked out into the bright morning light. Across from the sound stage was a row of portable dressing rooms shaped like big gray boxes. On one of them my name, written in felt pen on a slip of paper, was stuck to the door.

Inside Vivian said, "God, I remember when you used to have a trailer on the set. When they thought you had a chance to make it big."

She sat down on the sofa. I took the chair at the built-in makeup table.

"What do you want, Vivian?"

"I want to apologize for my behavior in the car yesterday. I've lived my life totally obsessed with Gordon and with you. I know he's had other affairs. But you were the first. The first to hurt me."

"I never went to bed with ..."

"Let me finish. I even became a blonde because of you. God, how he talked about you. It's ironical that you should be the one to remove my obsession. I want to thank you for that."

"For what?"

"For killing him," she said in a low voice.

"I didn't kill him."

"I don't want you to admit it. The police think it's suicide. That's fine with me."

"What kind of game are you playing, Vivian? You telephoned me last night and called me a slut and a murderer."

"No, I didn't."

"Too drunk to remember?"

"I was cold sober last night. For the first time in my life I didn't need booze or pills to sleep. I didn't need Gordon. I couldn't see what the bastard was like in life, but in death I could suddenly see him for what he was. That's why I wanted to thank you."

"Stop thanking me, Vivian."

"Look at me, Diana." She took off her sunglasses. Her eyes were bright and clear. Perfectly made up. "Do I look like the grieving widow? Do I look like somebody who was up drinking and making phone calls in the middle of the night? I only wore these dark glasses because I thought it was appropriate. I had one of the best nights of sleep I've ever had."

"If you didn't call me then who did?"

"Ask Wynn. She used to call Gordon and imitate my voice. Pretend she was me and tell him I/she was going to kill him. Then she'd break up laughing."

"How do you know this?"

"Gordon told me. He told me everything. That's how I knew about you and him. He told me how you liked it. How you would moan and scream out."

"I never went to bed with him, Vivian."

"It's all right, Diana. You don't have to lie. Gordon told me how Wynn likes it. He told me everything about her. You know, I never really enjoyed sex. Gordon was a man who tired of what he had and always desired what he didn't have. I thought that made us perfect for one another. Except he started to use his affairs against me. Tell me about them. In defense I made myself blonde, and for a while I tried to be what he wanted. A dirty blonde. But let's face it, I'm just a brunette with a low libido." Vivian laughed. "I have to be going. And again, thanks."

"Were you in Gordon's private bathroom yesterday?"

"No."

"You should've said yes, Vivian."

She studied me for a moment then left.

Tired, I lay down on the sofa. Maybe Gordon did kill himself. Maybe men become just as tired as women. But Vivian was in that bathroom and she lied about it. Why? There was a knock.

"Come in," I said, not moving.

"I hope I'm not disturbing you." Wynn peered down at me. Under her heavy layer of makeup I could see dark circles below her eyes.

"I was up all night trying to memorize my lines." She peered at herself in the mirror. "I look awful."

I sat up. "Don't try so hard to memorize. It's the worst thing an actor can do. Just keep reading the scene over and over, the lines will come."

"I can't concentrate. Will you help me? Can I come by tonight?" She looked so young and needy.

"Sure. Come by around eight."

"I keep thinking of Gordon in your car." She spoke to her reflection. "All that blood."

"Vivian told me that sometimes you pretended to be her and call Gordon and threaten him."

"It was just a joke. I realized I could imitate her voice. So I called up and tried it out on him." Another giggle. "Oh God, did he fall for it. It was the only time I could ever make him squirm."

"Did you call me last night and pretend to be Vivian?"

She licked her lips. "I need more gloss. Why would I pretend to be Vivian with you?"

"Maybe you wanted to make me squirm, too."

"I already did that, didn't I?"

"When?"

"In wardrobe yesterday. Gordon told me to strut around in front of you. He wanted you to see what he was getting now."

"And you didn't mind doing that?"

"I've done worse."

"Like what?"

"Other women, other guys. Whatever Gordon wanted." She kept watching herself in the mirror as she talked.

I stood behind her. Now we were both reflected in the mirror. There was an eerie resemblance. But her eyes and her mouth had a hardness that mine would never have.

"What does your boyfriend think of you doing things like that?"

"I never told him."

"Gordon wanted you to stop seeing your friend?"

"Yes. If I didn't stop he said he wouldn't help me."

"When you found Gordon and me in the car you said, 'Oh, my God, oh, my God' and then screamed."

"So?"

"That's my exact line in the script down to the scream."

"Those writers must know what they're doing because it's what people really say. Look, I'm the only one who had everything to lose by Gordon's death. Just remember that."

"Maybe you got tired of doing whatever Gordon wanted."

"Miss Poole, we're ready for you on the set. Is Wynn in there?" the third assistant director asked through the closed door.

"Yes, she is."

"We're ready for her, too."

"You're Miss Poole and I'm just Wynn. One day they'll call me by my last name."

"I think it has to do more with my age than being treated like a star. Do you really think Gordon killed himself?"

"I think I'm not a dirty blonde anymore. Like my new color? Golden blonde. And I'm going to see to it I stay golden."

I stood in the shower and watched the pinky-beige makeup run off my face and body and swirl down the drain. It was like washing away a second skin. I got out and wrapped myself in a white terry-cloth robe.

The doorbell rang. It was only 7:30. Wynn didn't strike me as a young woman who was ever early. As I made my way to the foyer the Mexican pavers in the living room and hall felt cold and smooth under my bare feet. I opened the door.

Detective Lang was wearing another cheap suit.

"Have you come to arrest me?"

He grinned. It was a nice grin. "No arrest. I wanted to give you this." He handed me a new package of pantyhose. My size. My color. "The others got a run in them."

I laughed. "Thanks. You sure you're not keeping them? I may be famous for fifteen minutes again."

"Let's hope it's longer this time."

"Has justice been served?" I asked.

"There were only Gordon Keith's fingerprints on the gun." He shrugged. "Let's say the powers that be have been served."

"Vivian lied to me. Said she wasn't in the bathroom."

"She said the same thing to me."

"Why lie about something so simple? If she had used his bathroom it wouldn't have proved anything."

"People get nervous and they lie."

"What about my car?"

He handed me a card. "Call this number. The only problem is you'll have to pay to have it cleaned and detailed. Well, it was nice to see you in person after all these years."

"Sorry you didn't score in the drive-in."

"I've gotten a little better at it since then. I just don't take my dates to see any of your old movies." I watched him as he retreated down the stone path.

I changed into jeans and a white cotton shirt. I had thought of putting on my warm-ups, but my ego was such that I couldn't sit around in baggy sweats while Wynn vamped in her mini.

At eight thirty she came in wearing a black short skirt and tight black sweater. "God, I'm sorry I'm late," she blurted.

"I didn't expect you to be on time."

She followed me into the living room. Her heels clicked on the pavers creating that same sharp staccato sound that only women in high heels make. Only women. I stopped. I had never heard the sound of Wynn's heels echoing on the concrete. She had just appeared by my car.

"Where's your script, Wynn?"

"Script?" She nervously clutched her purse to her flat belly.

"We were going to go over our lines together."

"I left it at home."

I felt uneasy. Even afraid. I moved toward the sliding glass doors that overlooked the deck and the ocean. I could see the shadowy figure on the beach walking the poodle again. If I screamed he might be able to hear me. That is, if he wasn't too close to the water. I started to open the doors.

"What are you doing?" she asked sharply.

"Letting in some air," I said, unlocking them.

"Don't."

"You were already in the garage, weren't you, Wynn?"

"Yes."

"What were you doing?" My heart was beginning to pound.

"I called Gordon and told him you were going to take me home. He went with me down to your Jag. He wanted you to see us together in your car." She giggled, then turned somber. "I didn't want to. I didn't want to be used anymore."

"Detective Lang was just here and told me the investigation is closed. Why don't we leave it at that?"

"You think we should leave it?" she asked.

"Yes, Wynn. Why don't you go home now?"

"No! I can't."

The doorbell rang. I started toward the foyer.

"Don't answer it," she yelled, fumbling in her purse. "Don't! I have a gun."

I lunged for the door and wrenched it open. Vivian Keith stood there.

"Hello, Diana. May I come in?"

She pushed past me into the living room. Wynn stood in the middle of the floor waving her gun looking like a child who had just been awakened from her sleep.

"I told you not to answer it," she said, the gun shaking in her hand. "I knew she was following me."

"Put it down, Wynn," I coaxed.

"That's right, Wynn, put it down." Vivian reached in her jacket pocket and came out with her own gun.

I stepped back. Too many women. Too many guns.

"It's not real," Wynn shouted. "It's not real."

Vivian fired. Wynn's knees buckled. She crumpled to the floor, rolled on her back, drawing up her knees. Moaning, her long legs slid straight out and she never moved again.

"She was trying to blackmail me," Vivian explained. "Comes to my home tonight and wants money. Starts waving that stupid fake gun around like she was Joan Crawford."

"You killed Gordon."

"She saw me do it. She was hiding behind some damn car."

"How did you know Gordon was going to be in the garage?" I asked, moving slowly backward toward the patio doors.

"I was in his office. As you said, I had gone into the bathroom." She moved with me. "I heard him on the phone. I thought he was talking to you. Going to meet you in your car. I knew he kept a gun in his desk. It was easy. I really had intended to kill you both. But you didn't show right away, and I couldn't stand there forever with a gun in my hand. So I made it look like suicide."

"Why kill Gordon after all these years?"

"To quote Oscar Wilde, 'The older women get, the angrier they get.' I'm very angry, Diana."

She aimed her gun. I felt the wind and smelled the ocean. There was a loud clatter on the deck. A big black poodle bounded into the room through the open patio doors. I lunged for Vivian knocking her off balance. We fell to the floor, the gun hard between our bodies. It went off. Her body jerked and again I felt warm blood on my skin. Her angry eyes widened.

"You okay?" Lang stood there with his legs wide apart, gun in hand, wearing a windbreaker over his cheap suit. Wagging its pom-pom tail the poodle loped around from Wynn, to Vivian, to me and back to him.

"Nice dog," I said getting to my feet.

"Belongs to my ex. I couldn't walk the beach at all hours without some kind of cover. Thought the dog fit right in. You know, Hollywood and all."

"You knew this was going to happen?"

"I knew she killed her husband. But I couldn't prove it. I just wanted to make sure that she didn't kill the other person she was obsessed with. You."

"You could have gotten here a little sooner."

"The damn dog broke loose. I had to chase it. Don't want the ex upset. Don't touch anything." He moved to the phone on the desk.

I peered down at Vivian. "I never went to bed with Gordon," I told her for the last time.

Over the years I have been to a few Hollywood parties and sometimes I leave wanting to commit murder. As my husband and I drove away from one of these in-your-face affairs, I said in an exhausted voice, "another tented evening." He looked at me and said, "That's a title for a short story." And so it was.

ANOTHER TENTED EVENING

Maurice Hamlin peered out from the party tent which covered a grassy section of his vast backyard. His shrewd eyes came to an uneasy rest on the Ferris wheel. It spun around in a blur of colorful lights. Well dressed men and bejeweled women seem to sit as high as the moon in their swaying chairs. They laughed and waved to one another with that slight embarrassment adults feel when they think they should be enjoying themselves more than they really are.

Disgusted, Hamlin turned his assessing gaze back to the interior of the tent and surveyed the frolicking clowns, the mimes frozen in mocking imitations of his guests, the balloon sellers, the cotton candy vendors, and the white-jacketed waiters serving Moet & Chandon champagne.

Hamlin had a familiar look in his eyes; the look of a producer whose movie has gone over budget and out of control. It was an expression I had seen many times in my years of being an actress. But this was not one of Hamlin's movies, this was his wife's fortieth birthday party.

"It's costing me a fortune. Where the hell is she, Diana?" he demanded.

"It's an important birthday. It's not easy for some women," I spoke from experience.

"The party's been going on for almost an hour. Robin's the one who wanted all this shit."

He tilted his round head toward me. His hair was obviously dyed a reddish-brown color. Hamlin didn't stay up nights worrying about the loss of subtlety in his search for youth, money, and a box-office hit.

"Oh, God, I can't believe I'm married to a forty year old woman." He eyed a lithe redhead swaying past him. A blue balloon was tied by a long string to the thin silvery strap of her low-cut dress. Printed on the balloon was HAPPY BIRTHDAY ROBIN.

"Will you go hurry her up, Diana?"

He didn't wait for an answer. Producers never do.

"I hope Robin doesn't sing tonight," he mumbled, walking quickly away to catch up with the young woman. I couldn't remember her name but she had done two movies and was poised to "make it big" or to disappear. It was another tented evening in Hollywood.

I made my way across the sparkling, black, AstroTurf, grabbed two glasses and a champagne bottle from a waiter's tray, and stepped out of the tent.

"Diana!"

It was Joyce Oliphant. She had just been named head of Horizon Studios. I knew her, many years ago, when she and I were the last of the starlets.

"Congratulations, Joyce."

"I didn't know you'd be here." She meant: *I thought you were out of the business and no longer important enough to be invited to the Hamlins'.*

Forcing her thin lips into a smile, she purposely did not introduce me to the men standing on each side of her. This was not just a lack of good manners. This was intended to intimidate, to make me feel ill at-ease. Their eyes hunted the party for more important people.

"What are you doing with yourself?" She tossed her highlighted-brown hair back from her lined, tense face. Her hair was too long for her age. It's difficult for some women to let go of the decade of their youth – ours was the sixties – no matter how successful they were in the present.

"I've got a small role in Hamlin's next picture," I said.

"I heard you had gone back to work. I do miss Colin."

And once again I felt that sharp, isolating pain of loss. Colin was my husband. He had died of a heart attack just fourteen months ago.

"I miss his wit," Joyce continued. "Where has all the wit gone?" Her greedy eyes searched the yard as if she could pluck wit from one of the guests' heads. "Colin had it. There are times, Diana, when a script isn't working, I want to pick up the phone and say get me Colin Hudson, the greatest writer Hollywood ever had."

"I wish you could," I said.

One of the men whispered in her ear. New prey had been found and she and I had talked too long. A conversation at a Hollywood party should not last over thirty seconds.

"We'll talk. God, I hope Robin doesn't sing tonight." Her Chanel shoulder bag, dangling on a gold and leather strap, hit me in the stomach as she spun away.

I was a middle-aged woman, still good looking enough for a middle-aged woman who was starting over in a business meant for very young women. I had no choice but to work. Colin and I had spent everything he had earned. No regrets. Besides, I had three things in my favor: I could act, I had contacts, and I knew how to play the game.

The Ferris wheel turned and the music blared as I made my way up the veranda steps to the enormous Neo-Mediterranean house which curved like a lover's arm around a mosaic-lined pool.

"Hello, Diana." Oscar Bryant, my ex-business manager, stood smoking a cigar. Next to him, lurking in the shadow of a banana palm, was Roland Hays the director.

"How are you, Oscar?"

"Still hoping you'll go out with me."

Dating your ex-business manager would be like dating your ex-gynecologist. He knows too much about your internal affairs.

"You know Roland Hays, don't you?" He turned to Hays. "This is Diana Poole."

The director was a slight man with receding black hair. He had a talent for getting the studios to make his movies even though they never turned a profit. For this reason he was referred to as an artist. His evasive dark eyes almost looked at me.

"Colin Hudson's widow," Oscar explained my existence.

"Great writer," the director muttered. "God, I hope Robin doesn't sing tonight."

"Why?" I asked.

"Have you ever heard her sing?" Oscar asked.

"No."

"Wait. Wait." He stared at the glasses and champagne bottle in my hands. "What's all that?"

"Robin's having trouble making an entrance."

He opened the French door for me. "Maybe you should just leave her up there." He chuckled.

"Better for all of us." The director stepped further back into the sword-like shadows of the palm.

The house was eerily quiet in contrast to the noise outside. Contemporary art haunted the walls. My high heels clicked out their lonely female sounds as I made my way across a limestone floor to the stairs.

I'd met Robin Hamlin six months ago in acting class. I had gone back to brush up on the craft I had left when I married Colin. I have to admit – and these things are important to admit – I would not be walking up these stairs, and I would not have made friends with Robin in acting class, if she were not Maurice Hamlin's wife. I say these things are important to admit because at least I'm not lying to myself. Not yet, anyway. As I said, I know how to play the game.

There was a side to Robin that was spontaneous and delightful. There was the other side that was petulant, insensitive, and demanding. But she had thought of me for the role in her husband's new movie and got me to read for him and the director. In Hollywood that makes her a person of character. There was also something poignant about Robin. At the age of forty she still dreamed, like a young girl dreams, of being a movie star, a performer, or just famous. Her husband had given her some small roles in his movies. And that's all they were – small roles doled out by a powerful husband to his wife.

I made my way down the long hallway to her bedroom suite.

"Robin? It's Diana," I announced to the closed door. "I come bearing champagne. Robin?" I waited. "Robin? Maurice is worried about you."

I tapped the door with my toe then pushed it with my foot. It opened. I stepped into a mirrored foyer. My blonde hair, black evening suit, one strand of pearls, red lips, reflected in a jagged kaleidoscopic maze.

"Robin? It's Diana."

A mirrored door opened. Robin stood there holding a sterling silver candelabra. Two of the four candles were missing. The ones that remained were tilted at a funny angle. Her black hair caressed her bare shoulders. The famous diamond and emerald necklace, which Maurice had given Robin for her last birthday, dazzled around her long slim neck. The necklace and the candelabra were her only attire.

"Nice outfit," I said.

"Thank God, Diana. Come in here quick."

I followed her into the bedroom. She locked the door. Setting the bottle and the glasses on her mauve, taffeta-skirted vanity I saw William DeLane reflected in the beveled mirror. Fully clothed, he leaned against the white velvet headboard. His misty gray eyes, full of surprise, stared into mine. I whirled around. The right side of his head was caved in. Blood splattered the white coverlet and his green jacket. Little drops of blood dotted the headboard near his thick brown hair. I didn't have to check his pulse to know he was dead. On the floor next to the bed was a white cocktail dress. Blood streaked the shimmering fabric.

"I ruined my dress." Robin stamped her foot. Her implanted breasts never moved.

"Jesus Christ, Robin, what happened?"

Her voice went off into a whine. "I'm not going to cry. I'm not going to cry." She took a deep breath and didn't cry.

I pried the candelabra from her hand and set it on a table between two lavender-striped chairs.

"It doesn't go there. It goes on the mantel." She gestured toward an ornate marble fireplace.

"Robin, that's William Delane." Delane was a young and very successful screenwriter.

"Don't you think I know that? At least give me credit for knowing who I killed. Nobody gives me credit."

"Let me get Maurice."

"No. Don't you dare." She grabbed a silk bathrobe off a chaise lounge, slipped it on, and sat down.

"I need to think this out." Her beautiful but remote violet-colored eyes studied me. "Delane said you two went out last week."

"We had dinner together." With a shaking hand I poured champagne into the two glasses and gave her one. "He wanted to talk with me because I was Colin's wife. Widow. He wanted to know how Colin lived and worked."

"Why?" She crossed her long bare legs. Perfectly manicured toes glistened red.

"I think he was searching for some kind of an example, or a mooring. Some sort of image to hold on to." I took a long swallow of the champagne and avoided Delane's shocked eyes.

"You mean like a father image?" she asked earnestly.

"More like a male muse. A creative guide in the jungle of Hollywood. He felt his success was based on sheer guts and ego."

"Isn't everyone's?" Her remote expression became more intent. "Did he talk about me?"

"Yes. He told me he was having an affair with you." His exact words were: 'I'm having an affair with Maurice Hamlin's wife.'

"But it wasn't enough, was it?"

"He was questioning his relationship to his success. Not his relationship with you," I said carefully, knowing that sex and success were so intermingled in Hollywood that it was difficult to discuss one without the other.

She turned and peered at Delane. "Why would anybody question success?"

I forced myself to look at him. God, he was so young and such a hack. There was a time when Hollywood turned talented writers into banal, soulless creatures. Now they arrived in town without souls. They arrived schooled in the cliché and eager to be rewritten.

"He's had three hit movies," I explained. "And he couldn't tell the difference between the first movie and the third movie. He felt that his words had no meaning. No connection to anything or anybody. Most of all they had no connection to himself. Why did you kill him, Robin?"

She didn't answer. I opened a pair of French doors that led out onto a narrow foot balcony. I could see the spinning Ferris wheel and hear the music and the laughter of the guests inside the tent. I took a deep breath and watched Maurice embracing a tree. I looked again. A blue balloon floated out from under a leafy limb. I realized that between him and the tree was the redheaded actress, whose chances for making it were looking better. I closed the doors.

"Delane sneaked up here to give me my birthday gift." Robin gestured toward a stack of leather-bound books piled on the floor near the bed. "The complete works of Ernest Hemingway."

"You killed him because he gave you the complete works of Ernest Hemingway?"

"No. But why give me some macho writer's books?"

"I think he was trying to give his own life some meaning."

"But why give me Hemingway's books? Do you see what I mean? Why me?" Her voice quivered. She stood and began to pace, stopped, thought a moment, then went to her closet and pulled out a yellow dress. She grabbed some pantyhose from a drawer.

"Do you remember who I was having an affair with on my last birthday?" she asked, wiggling into the pantyhose.

"I didn't know you then."

"Philip Vance."

Philip was a featured player. Not a star, not a character actor, but always working and always listed around fifth place in the credits.

"Do you know what he gave me for a present?" Robin pulled opened another drawer and took out a rhinestone pin from a small velvet box. The broach was in the shape of a heart with a ruby arrow piercing it.

"It's cheap but I love it," she said, sounding like a teenage girl.

I knew the pin well. Philip had given me one fifteen years ago. I never wore it. Philip had been giving out these rhinestone pins for twenty years and always with the same line: "I can't afford diamonds but the heart is real."

He counted on the expensive taste of his conquests. Knowing his *ladies*, as he called them, would never wear anything so obviously inexpensive, he was free to give the same pin to his next *lady*.

"It's not that I have to have anything expensive," Robin said. "Just something that's sentimental. Something that means I was loved. 'I can't afford diamonds but the heart is real.' " She stared sadly at the pin, then tucked it lovingly back into the drawer.

"Do you remember when we were in acting class together?" she asked, stepping into the yellow dress.

"Yes."

"And Rusty our teacher told us to close our eyes and tell him what we saw? What we imagined? Do you remember what you saw?"

"No."

"A bird with a broken wing on a flagstone patio. A man's wrist and the sleeve of his white shirt turned back. Do you remember what I saw?"

"No."

"Nothing. I saw nothing. And then Rusty asked me to describe the nothingness. Remember?"

"Yes?"

"And I asked how can I describe nothing? I mean, you can't. The closest I could come was a sort of a grayish black. Nothing is nothing. Zip me up."

I zipped her up.

"Oh, God, I didn't want to wear this." She turned on Delane's corpse as if he had commented on her dress. "He made me feel like nothing. I suddenly could see it. Feel it."

"How did he do that, Robin?"

"He just couldn't believe that when all was said and done, he was a writer who was having an affair with his producer's wife. I could handle that. But he couldn't. So he tried to make it more than it was. And he tried to change me. That's when he made me feel like nothing." She put on some lipstick and smoothed her hair.

"Change you into what?"

"He blamed Maurice for everything. He said it was his money and power that kept me from truly knowing who I was. I told him he was crazy that he was talking about himself. Not me. I told him it was over. That I didn't want to see him anymore." She stared defiantly at herself in the mirror. "I turned forty today and told a man I didn't want him. I didn't need him anymore."

She sat back down on the lounge and slipped her feet into bright yellow high heels.

"Then it should've been a great night. Why didn't it just end there?" I poured her another glass of champagne.

"Because as I was leaving to go down to the party he said, 'Please, do us all a favor and don't sing tonight.' "

She tapped her long red nails against the glass, took another sip, and then slowly peered at Delane.

"Why didn't he want you to sing?" I asked.

"He said people laugh when I sing. I've never heard anybody laugh, Diana. I told him that. He was lying on the bed just like he is now. I was standing by the fireplace. He said it was an uneasy laughter. That if I sang I would remind my guests of how untalented they really are. And how much money they earn for being so untalented. I grabbed the candelabra, turned, and swung it at his head. Not just once, but a couple of times." Her eyes moved from Delane to me. "You're going to call the police, aren't you?"

"Yes."

"But not till after I sing. Promise?"

"All right."

She stood, downed the last of her champagne, and walked slowly out of the room.

I poured myself another glass, opened the French doors, and stepped out onto the narrow foot balcony. I looked toward the tree. Maurice and the redhead were gone. Robin appeared on the verandah. She stopped and looked up in my direction and waved. I waved back. The emerald and diamond necklace shone like glass. Guests began to move toward her, surrounding her as if she were a movie star and not just another wife who had turned forty. They all disappeared into the tent.

The caterers wheeled a giant cake out onto the verandah. It blazed like a small brush fire. Christ, Maurice had them put all forty candles on the cake. They lifted it off the cart and carried it into the tent. A hush fell. I could hear applause then guests singing Happy Birthday. The Ferris wheel went around in a garish blur, its now empty carriages swaying under the cold eye of the moon. There was another hush. Then the sound of a piano. And soon Robin's voice wafted up through the tent into the night sky. I didn't know the song. Some rock ballad. She hit all the right notes, but she had a thin, wavering, unfeeling voice. Delane was right. She was relentlessly untalented. But not any worse than some others who have made it on just sheer guts and ego. Not any worse than Delane.

The tent reminded me of an evangelist's tent. A place where people come to be told there is another world. A better world. Where people can believe that Hollywood will save them no matter what they do or how they do it. Her pathetic voice, unintentionally, questioned that belief.

I moved back into the room and again forced myself to look at the body of the young, successful Delane. I couldn't bear the surprised look in his eyes. After three hit movies his words had finally connected. I pulled the white silk coverlet over his face.

I was so tired of hearing the hype about the sixties that I wanted to kill the decade off just to give other generations a chance at defining themselves. Alas that doesn't make a short story. It wasn't until I heard that a rock star my husband and I knew from that decade had had a liver transplant. I began to wonder what would happen if a debauched aging rock star received a new liver; and what if he began to believe that his healthy organ would allow him to regain the success he had as a wild rock star in the sixties. I now had my theme and my story.

KILLING THE SIXTIES

What do you wear to meet an ex-lover who is now an aging rock star with a new liver? Well, a used liver, but new to him.

I decided on my blood-red linen dress.

The last time I saw Leon Ashe was in Chasen's about ten years ago, just before the restaurant closed for good. He was drunk and in a fight with the maitre d' over the location of his table. As the waiters dragged Leon unceremoniously out of the restaurant he spotted me sitting on the banquette with my husband. "Diana!" he yelled. Then in his plaintive drunken voice he began singing the song he had written about me in the sixties; it was appropriately named "Diana," and its success had made him a giant rock star.

I didn't see him or hear from him again until last week, when he called to announce that he had a new liver. He asked if I'd come up to Oak Point, where he now lived, and spend the day with him. He suggested I meet him at a restaurant called Avanti. I was between movies, as most middle-aged actress are, and with some coaxing on his part I agreed to drive up the coast to see him.

The reason I needed coaxing was because I never trusted Leon Ashe, even when I was madly in love with him back in the sixties. Leon thought of women the way he thought of the songs he wrote: the next one was always going to be Number One. The trouble with Leon is that "Diana" was the best song he ever wrote. You can hear it today in elevators and if you're holding on the phone. Funny how time equalizes everything. After all these years, the significance, the genius of Leon Ashe is reduced to muzak. An outcome he never anticipated in the sixties.

There was another reason I hesitated to see Leon: He always had an ulterior motive. Leon wanted something. I knew one thing he wouldn't want – to be lovers again. I'm too old for Leon now, even though I'm ten years younger than he is. His current and fifth wife is twenty-two. But, as I said, I had time on my hands, and despite everything, I always had a soft spot for Leon. After all, he wrote a beautiful love song for me when I was a tearful eighteen-year-old girl.

Montecito is an expensive little village, nestled between the San Ysidro Mountains and the Pacific Ocean, just south of Santa Barbara. From my home in Malibu it took me about an hour and half to get there. The village consists of small shops, four or five Italian restaurants, and homes worth millions and millions of dollars. Many Hollywood people have moved up to Montecito to get away. But I've been around long enough to know that you can't get away from Hollywood. Like smog, Hollywood moves and settles wherever it wants to. It doesn't matter if you're a success or a failure, you're always breathing it, living it, hoping for just one more chance from it. In other words, while the Hollywood people were retreating to Montecito, they were still waiting for the phone to ring.

Avanti is a small, comfortably chic outdoor restaurant. I parked the car, smoothed my blood-red dress, combed my determinedly blonde hair, put on some fresh lipstick, and went into the patio area.

Shadowed from the sun by market umbrellas, the Montecetans were busy eating. The women, mostly middle-aged, were lean, taunt, and as determinedly blonde as I. The men had an air of robustness about them that comes more from money than fitness. Behind them the San Ysidro Mountains rose in jagged grandeur. Clouds carved ragged white holes into a brilliant blue sky.

"Diana? Diana Poole!" Leon stood when he saw me.

"Hello, Leon."

We embraced. Then, holding me at arms length, he leaned his head back, squinted as if I were a newspaper he was trying to read without glasses, and said, "You look great."

It's the one compliment that fits all middle-aged women, and because of that it irritates the hell out of me.

"So does the Grand Canyon, Leon," I laughed.

"What?" he muttered, distractedly, eyeing a lone man sitting at a table, reading a newspaper.

"You're looking well," I said.

"Feel wonderful. Sit down. Sit down."

His once shoulder-length black hair was now gray and shaggy. His dark beard was only a memory, but his eyes were still the color of glistening oil. His deeply lined face was thinner, causing his aquiline nose to appear larger. He wore a perfectly pressed blue work shirt and jeans. His black sports jacket was cashmere.

"God, I can't tell you how good it is to see you, Diana." He smiled his charmingly crooked smile.

"It's been a long time." I smiled back.

"But that's going to change."

"What is?"

"Now that your husband is dead. Oh, I'm sorry to hear about that by the way. I should have written you. When did it happen?" He talked fast. His dark, furtive eyes roamed the patio. He wanted to get the subject of death over with.

"More than a year ago." Again the feeling of being set adrift from everything I knew and loved swept through me. Waiting for it to pass,

I looked up at the mountains; the clouds had lowered and were trying to drape themselves over its peaks and ridges. The feeling of loss ebbed and I let my gaze drift back to Leon. For the first time I noticed the half-empty bottle of white wine.

"I saw you in that movie," he announced, "where you played Uma Thurman's mother. Kind of a small role for you, wasn't it?"

"It gets tougher the older you get."

"It doesn't have to." He poured himself a glass of wine. "Is Uma seeing anyone?"

"You asked me to come all the way up here to find out if Uma Thurman is seeing someone?" I joked.

"I just wondered, that's all." His voice was serious. "Possibilities, you know what I mean?"

The waiter swooped by, tossed menus on the table, and poured me a glass of wine.

"We'll have another bottle," Leon ordered.

"Should you be drinking?" I asked when the waiter left.

"I have a second chance at life, Diana," he said, excitedly.

"That's wonderful. But I thought that drinking and drugs is what got to your liver in the first place. I remember when you were on stage and told everybody in the audience to drop acid."

"But that's just it. I'm gonna do it all over again, Diana. Well, not acid. Though I think for a short period it did make me more creative. Back then I would've tried anything to be more creative."

"Do what all over again?"

"I'm going to live my life over. How many people get that chance?" He downed his wine. "It took me thirty-some years to need a transplant, so I figure I have another thirty years before this one gives out. Then it won't matter. Who wants to live past eighty?" he asked, sounding like the young Leon I had once loved.

"I remember when we didn't want to live past thirty. I don't think that's the way it works, Leon. Do your doctors know you're drinking?"

With a suspicious glance he leaned close and whispered, "Is that guy staring at me?"

"What guy?" I looked around.

"Jesus, Diana, don't be so obvious. He's sitting alone. Pretending to read his newspaper." He sneaked a peek. "He's not watching me now. You can look."

I peered at a man who was about Leon's age sitting at a table for two. He had a slight belly, thinning grayish-blond hair, and was dressed in khakis and a baby-blue polo shirt. After sipping his beer he patted his neatly trimmed mustache and seemed to be thoroughly engrossed in *The Wall Street Journal.*

"He *is* reading his newspaper, Leon."

"The doctors say this happens with a transplant. It's a kind of temporary paranoia. You know, you feel guilty for getting to live while the others ..." He paused, shifting restlessly in his chair.

"Others what?"

"Others on the list. The ones that didn't get the liver, the ones who've been waiting a long time." He tossed back some more wine. "Let's face it, it helps to have a name, it helps to have money. I took advantage of that. Why shouldn't I? I was dying. People wanted me to live. I wrote some great songs, man. They still love me for that. I was part of their youth. No, I helped create their youth, their memories. That's why I want to start writing again. I owe it to them." He slammed his hand on the table. A sparrow scavenging for bread crumbs flew away. A few heads turned. The man reading the *Journal* never looked up.

"That's why I wanted to see you, Diana. You were there when it all started for me. Remember?" He grinned charmingly and poured the rest of the bottle into his glass.

"Of course I do."

"I was sitting at the bar in Martoni's."

Martoni's was a restaurant located near the recording studios in Hollywood. In the sixties it became a hangout for the music people.

"You were with some guy," he said. "You were crying."

"Yes, I'd just broken up with him. God, what was his name? I can't even remember why we were angry at one another."

"He wanted to marry you, Diana."

"That's right. And I wanted to be an actress. I was only eighteen, the last thing I wanted was marriage. What was his name?"

"His name doesn't matter."

"Jack! Jack ... .something. God, I thought I would never forget him. What was his last name?"

"He's not important," Leon said testily. "It's what happened that's important, Diana. I had been watching you from the bar."

"Jack. Jack ... God, I almost had it."

"Forget the last name. You got up and went to the restroom. He got up and left the restaurant. I couldn't believe a guy could leave anyone so beautiful as you. You looked like Marianne Faithful."

"Even Marianne Faithful looked like Marianne Faithful in those days. When I returned to the table you were sitting in Jack's place. I was still crying. And without saying anything you handed me your handkerchief. No, your bandanna. It was a very touching gesture."

"And then I asked you your name, remember?"

"And I told it to you."

"And while you cried I wrote the lyrics for a song on the back of a cocktail napkin. I wanted to cheer you up."

"Very sad words for a very sad young woman."

"I want to do it again," he declared.

"Do what again?"

"Your husband is dead which is similar to that guy walking out on you," he attempted to explain.

"It's not similar at all, Leon."

He leaned back in his chair and asked, "Why did you marry Colin anyway?"

"I loved him." What an inadequate phrase. Why does it always sound defensive?

"You loved me. And?"

"And what?"

"What other reason?"

"He never cheated one me," I teased.

"How do you know?" He smiled.

"I know."

"I cheated on you. And?"

"And I loved the way he wrote. I loved his words." Colin was a screenwriter and novelist. I have his two Oscars on the mantle. They are cold and heavy.

"And you never loved my words except for that one song. In fact, you stopped loving me when it became a hit. Left me just when I needed you the most," Leon complained.

"After you wrote 'Diana' you became terribly self-destructive."

"We were all self-destructive in the sixties."

"Not all of us. Just what do you want to do again, Leon?"

"I want to write you a song. Like I did in Martoni's."

We stared at one another. He was grinning, eager. I wasn't. I was feeling uncomfortable.

"Well, that's very sweet, Leon, but ..."

"Sweet? Sweet! It's not sweet. All my other songs were never as good, were they? I mean it was my voice that made all those stupid lyrics I wrote sound meaningful. My whole career, I kept trying to equal that one damn song. Every time I had a new album out it was compared to 'Diana.' "

"It happens."

"It didn't happen to the Beatles," he barked.

"Let me get this straight. You want to write me a new song. A song as good as the old one so you can have a number-one record again. You don't need me for that. Go do it."

Abruptly his mood shifted. "Every time I saw you up on the screen you reminded me of that song, and that you left me," he accused, furious.

"You left me. For another woman."

"I thought she would spark something in me the way you had. Only better. What was her name?"

"It doesn't matter." It was my turn to be testy.

"We always argued, didn't we?" he said, sadly.

"Yes." I sighed.

"I just want to write one more great song. Is that such a terrible thing? And I want to do it with you, because you were there." Excited, he grabbed my arm. "I know I can have another hit." His jacket fell open, and I could see a gun in a holster attached to the side of his waist band.

"A gun?" I blurted.

"WHERE!" Leon jerked around in his chair. Another bird flew. A few more heads turned.

Lowering my voice, I said, "Attached to your waistband, Leon."

"Jesus Christ, don't do that, Diana. You scared the hell out of me." Hand shaking, he emptied his glass. Then he added, defensively, "I have a permit."

"To own a gun? Or to carry it on you?"

"How the hell do I know? Who reads the small print?"

"What are you afraid of, Leon?" I tried to keep my voice calm.

"I'm not paranoid," he protested. "I know that's what the doctors think. Temporary paranoia. But it's not true. Look around you. This isn't the world you and I grew up in. It's changed."

I looked around. Their stomachs filled with pasta and wine, the Montecetans leaned comfortably back in their deck chairs. The sun had lowered, the clouds had turned an unexplainable pink. The mountains were becoming a soft purple.

"Leon you're living in one of the wealthiest, safest communities there is. That's what's changed."

"Someone wants me dead," he said flatly, reaching into his pocket for a crumbled piece of paper.

He handed it to me. Large letters, cut from a glossy magazine, were glued to the paper forming the sentence: YOU TOOK MY LIFE.

"When did you get this?"

"Soon after I moved up here. It was just left in the mail box. Someone knows where I live."

"Were there other messages?"

"Two more over the last six months saying the same thing." His gaze darted to the lone man, who was now eating a bowl of Santa Barbara mussels.

"Why isn't that guy with somebody?"

"Maybe he's waiting for someone."

"But he's already eating. Nobody eats alone in this town. You can drink alone, but you can't eat alone. Don't you see?"

"See what?"

"Maybe it's him."

"Leon, he's just a man having lunch. Settle down, please."

"I can't. What if I took his wife, or daughter or son? Maybe he had a loved one on the list. Maybe I got the organ that was to go to someone he loved."

"That's all kept private. They don't tell people those things. No one could know ..."

"You can find out anything you want to in this world, Diana, if you have the money and the need."

"Hey Leon, my man!" A short round man in his twenties, wearing a black coat, black silk shirt with no collar, black slacks, black woven slippers, and earrings, patted Leon's back. "How ya doing? I just came up from L.A."

"Steve!" Leon leapt to his feet and began pumping Steve's hand.

Steve turned to his companion and gushed, "Leon Ashe. The legend." His companion nodded vaguely, watching their waiting table.

"How come you didn't return my phone call?" Leon demanded.

"We'll talk, Leon." Steve edged quickly away. He and his friend sat down near the man who was eating alone.

"Do you know who that is?" Leon settled back in his chair. I shook my head.

"Steve Tinker. The number-one record producer. He's got three records in the top ten. I remember when I had two. He called me when he heard I was dying. Said how much I'd formed his views on music. Said he wished that he'd had a chance to work with me. Said he wouldn't be where he was today if I hadn't made the records I'd made. Especially, 'Diana.' " Leon stopped talking and lapsed into an uneasy silence. The lines deepened around his mouth, and he began to nod his head as if he'd just figured out something.

"I didn't die, Diana," he said harshly. "I lived. I called Steve Tinker back to see when he wanted to work with me. But he never returned my phone calls. Not one. I'm tired of being a fucking legend, Diana. I'm gonna show them. I'm gonna do it again. But I need you." He was pleading now.

"What do I have to do with any of this, Leon?"

"You were, you *are* 'Diana.' Don't you see? You were better than acid."

"How's your wife?"

"Young. She doesn't even know who Three Dog Night is. You don't think I can do it again, do you?"

"I think you don't *have* to do it again, Leon."

"I gotta take a leak." He jumped up and loped a wide circle around the lone man, who was busy plucking a mussel from its shell.

I took a sip of wine and for a brief moment wondered what my life would have been like if I had married Jack what's-his-name. He didn't want me to be an actress. I remembered that. So I would've ended up the wife of an insurance salesman? A banker? To me, Jack had represented what we were all afraid of in the sixties. Stability. He was hard-working. Earnest. But there was something about him, something I had responded too. What? I couldn't remember. And what were we doing in Martoni's? I must've taken him there. I was young and wanted to be a part of The Scene. And then I met Leon. Now, Leon wants to go back to that time, that moment. Or does he just want to be young again, and not afraid of death?

The number-one record producer got up and came toward me. "You a friend of Leon's?" he asked urgently.

"Yes."

"I did a good deed and called a dying man expecting ..." He paused, dabbing at his small lips with his napkin, trying to find the right words.

"Expecting him to die?" I helped.

"Yes. So tell him to stop calling me. Or I'm going to start taking those calls of his as threats, as a form of stalking." He made an attempt at looking thoughtful and asked, "Didn't I just see you in something? You played Uma Thurman's mother in *Like Daughter*. You were great."

"Bette Davis was great."

"Is she seeing anybody?" he asked.

"Bette Davis?"

"Uma Thurman."

"Yes."

"Tell Leon to lay off." He clamped shut his small petty lips, stopped to shake someone else's hand, and returned to his table.

Leon did his unintentionally funny lope around the lone man, who was now dipping bread in his broth, and sat down opposite me.

"Where's the other bottle of wine?" he asked rubbing his hands together.

"I'm hungry. Let's eat."

We got the waiter's attention, ordered lunch, and Leon got his new bottle.

Whispering, he asked, "Did you see the way he was looking at me?"

"The record producer?"

"The guy eating alone."

"He's not looking at you, Leon."

"He was."

"Maybe he knows who you are. Have you ever thought of that?"

"Why would he know?"

"Because you're a legend. Remember?"

"It's not that kind of look. He doesn't admire me. I can tell. I think I'm being followed."

"Did you go to the police with the messages?"

"What good are the police?" Not waiting for an answer, he quickly changed the subject back to us. "You and I may have argued, but we were magical together, Diana."

"We were miserable together, Leon. The minute your record came out and went to number one you changed. You lost your sense of humor, your wit. You spent your entire time, no your entire career, trying to recreate that one record."

"I was an artist."

"Stravinsky was an artist. Picasso was an artist."

"Are you saying I wasn't? Are you saying I didn't know what I was doing?" he exploded, a wild look appeared in his dark eyes. A few people turned.

I lowered my voice and tried to reassure him. "I'm saying you wrote one hell of a song. But you were a better performer. Your best hits were with other peoples' songs. You didn't need to write another 'Diana.' You still don't need to do that. Find some rock standards, record them. That's what you need to do. Go out and perform. Rock-and-roll, now, is middle-aged and sober. Stop drinking."

"You've never understood me, have you? It was the singer-songwriters who were the fucking artists. I didn't want to be some parrot mouthing other people's words. I forgot what kind of shrew you are. Even at eighteen you had a tongue dipped in venom."

"Pen."

"What?"

"Never mind."

"I didn't ask you to come here to give me reality checks. When I was dying all I could of think of was you. Thank God I lived so I could remember you as you really are. You haven't aged that well, Diana," he observed spitefully.

"At least I have my own liver," I snapped back.

"What do you mean by that?"

"It was a stupid reply to your attempt at a hurtful remark."

"No, you meant you're free from guilt. You meant you haven't taken something that really belongs to someone else. That's what you meant."

"I can't carry on this conversation anymore, Leon. I'm sorry, but we always end up hurting each other. I never should've come."

"No, you hurt me. I never hurt you," he persisted dangerously.

The lone man at the table stood, holding his paper he walked toward us.

"Excuse me, are you Leon Ashe?" he asked, slightly embarrassed.

Leon blanched. Trembling, he reached inside his sport coat, fumbling for his gun.

"Leon, don't." I grabbed hold of his arm. He shoved me away.

The man looked confused. "I just wanted to say that you wrote one of the greatest songs. You are Leon Ashe, aren't you?"

Leon pulled his gun out. But somehow he'd got it by the barrel. Attempting to get it pointed at the man, he knocked over the wine bottle: It shattered on the pavers. The man took a quick step back. The Montecetans began to move nervously in their chairs. Leon got the barrel pointed in the right direction. The man retreated some more.

"Leon, don't!" I screamed.

The sound of the gun cracked through the al fresco dining. Patrons ducked under their tables. Sunglasses flew, birds flew, wine glasses toppled.

"Leon!" I breathed in.

Still aiming the gun, Leon stood. The man froze. Then Leon dropped his gun, clutched his chest, and fell to the ground. The man let his newspaper fall, displaying his own gun. We looked briefly at one another as he placed it on the table and walked out to the parking lot.

"Call for help," I screamed, kneeling by Leon.

Blood ran from his mouth. His eyes were half open. I felt for a pulse. Leon Ashe was dead. The record producer was on his knees, waving his napkin as if he were surrendering. The customers, most of them flattened on the floor, began reaching for their wives, husbands, lovers, friends, sunglasses. I hurried out to the parking lot.

Eyes closed, the man leaned against a Range Rover. He clasped his hands tightly in front of him in a desperate kind of prayer. Sensing my presence, he slowly looked at me.

"Hello, Diana."

"Jack Hartford." I'd finally remembered the last name of the man who had left me in Martoni's all those years ago.

"I wrote you a poem on the back of a cocktail napkin." He spoke in calm quiet voice. "I left it for you on the table to let you know how much I loved you. I thought it would bring you back to me. That it would show you that I had more in me than just wanting to be a banker."

"You wrote the words to 'Diana'?"

"I was a romantic. Leon was a thief."

"But why kill him?"

"Leon got away with everything. Even my words. Even you. The day I read he was dying was one of the happiest days of my life. But then he got a liver transplant and moved to Montecito. I put messages in his mailbox to scare him. But I knew he wasn't going to leave. He destroyed my youth; I wasn't going to let him destroy my retirement. I read about your husband's death. I'm sorry."

"Thank you."

"My wife died recently."

"I'm sorry."

"Thank you."

"You grew a mustache."

"Yes. Lost most of my hair." He flushed. "I wanted to call you, Diana. Tell you I was really the romantic."

"Why didn't you?"

"Would you have believed me?"

"Not when I was eighteen. But now? Yes."

"He shot Leon Ash. A rock'n'roll legend," the record producer chanted to a group forming around us. "A fucking legend!" He still clutched his napkin, which was covered with marinara sauce or Leon's blood.

"I saw you play Uma Thurman's mother," Jack Hartford said, taking me in. You're still beautiful, Diana."

I put my hand on his cheek. He covered my hand with his.

"If only you'd called me," I said.

The police pulled up and got out of their cars. Without being commanded, Jack Hartford threw his arms in the air. It was a gesture worthy of the movies. Like leaving a poem on a table for a tearful young woman to discover.

I was pondering why some women have so much plastic surgery done to their faces. When they look in the mirror do they really think they look younger or better? Or as they now say, "rested." Then I remembered the phrase that all women at one time or another have blurted out, "God, I look like my mother." Then I asked myself the question: What if a woman feared looking like her mother to such an extent that that she would let, or be cajoled by, a plastic surgeon to work on her until she was unrecognizable, even to her friends? Now all I had to do was answer that question and I had a story.

FACING UP

"Movie stars should never have children, Diana," Ella Sands greeted me at the top of the dramatically curved stairs, which seemed to be designed for grand entrances and exits.

"Is that because we spend our lives acting like children?" I asked, hurrying up the steps.

"Because we're artists." Her famous voice was soft but sure. Seventy-five years had not reduced its seductive power, nor had it diminished the inherent beauty of the once famous star who had been an icon of her generation.

We went into her sitting room. She settled in a chair that had been intentionally placed under a portrait painted at the height of her career. The young, beautiful Ella peered down from her gilded frame with a slightly perplexed expression at the old woman she had become. Next to Ella a table lamp glowed with a soft pink light that smoothed her lines and the hollows around her eyes and illuminated her still beautiful auburn hair. Ella had controlled her image and her career, including the placement of chairs and lights, with an iron discipline. Brushing my determinedly blonde hair back from my face I sat across from her.

"I know I've become a bit Blanche Dubois...ish but what the hell I've earned it."

I laughed. "It's good to see you. It's been a long time." But I knew this wasn't a social call. It never was with Ella Sands. She only asked to see you when she wanted something.

"Did you know Kera got married? " Her sharp green eyes took me in.

"I heard." I couldn't keep the bitterness out of my voice.

"Doctor Logan Bradford. A plastic surgeon. Can you believe Kera married a plastic surgeon? That's like marrying your gynecologist. There's something obscene about it." She tossed her head back and laughed her I-just-got-out-of-bed-with-a-man laugh.

I forced a smile. "Somebody has to marry them."

"But not my daughter."

"I hear he's a brilliant plastic surgeon." I couldn't think of anything else to say.

"Do you remember the actor Farley Sims? He was brilliant too. When the camera was rolling I would have trusted Farley with my life. He was that good of an actor. But when the camera was off I never went near him because he hated women, he was duplicitous, and he'd walk over anyone who got in his way. Dr. Logan Bradford reminds me of Farley."

"I'm sorry." I didn't feel any sympathy for her daughter. I had never liked Kera. She and I were under contract to Universal Studios back in the seventies when we were both young and unknown. She seemed to think she was there by right, being the daughter of a star. She never bothered to learn her lines, or be on time, while I couldn't sleep for fear I'd be late for my makeup call. And if I did sleep I dreamed of being in front of the camera without ever having read the script.

"I think he's experimenting on her," Ella spoke in a whisper.

"Experimenting?"

"I don't recognize my daughter anymore. If you passed her on the street you wouldn't know her, Diana. My God, I've had my eyes done twice and my face lifted once. But I still look like me. I can't see myself in my daughter's face. Kera looks like *he* created her not *me*." Possession hardened her voice.

"Kera's a strong woman, Ella. Why does she allow it?"

"She was never strong. Just willful. I think she's afraid of him, for whatever reason, and because of that she's allowing him to mutilate her, destroy her. I can't stand looking at my own daughter." She reached out and pressed my hand in hers. "Talk to her, Diana. See if you can find out what kind of hold he has on her."

The last time I saw Kera she was in bed with my husband. That was ten years ago.

"You know that Kera and I haven't spoken in years," I replied. "I don't want to get involved with her."

She let my hand drop in my lap as if it had suddenly developed leprosy and leaned back in her chair staring at me imperiously. Movie stars are not used to being rejected, even if they are ex-movie stars. "If Colin were alive he would do it for me."

"Well, he's not." My husband had died a year ago of a heart attack leaving me with a mortgaged teardown in Malibu, an old Jaguar, two Oscars for Best Screenplay, and a sense of loss I could never fill.

"If I were still Number One at the box office you'd do it for me," she observed, unpleasantly.

"That's unfair even for you."

"It's reality. I think Kera's husband wants to kill me."

"What?"

"It's not an aging woman's paranoia, Diana."

"Why would he want to kill you?"

"Money. My jewels. The real estate I've invested in. This house. I wasn't like you and Colin who spent everything you had. I never spent a penny. I'm worth over forty million and it took a lifetime for me to do it. Today some stars earn that for one movie. My God, they don't know anything about acting and they make that kind of money."

"Logan Bedford must make a lot of money on his own, Ella."

"He owes people. He has always lived beyond his means."

"So he owes people. That doesn't mean he wants to harm you."

"You think I'm crazy? "

"No, I think you're trying anything to get me to reunite you with your daughter."

"I took a chance on your husband back in the seventies when he was a nobody. It was having me, Ella Sands, in his first movie, which put him on the map as a screenwriter." For emphasis she tapped a perfectly manicured finger just above her still abundant cleavage.

"Colin wasn't my husband then. And it was a brilliant script with or without you."

Suddenly her shoulders slumped and her face went slack making her look aged. "I'm an old woman, Diana," she pleaded dramatically.

I grinned. "You *are* a wonderful actress."

"I can see this isn't working." She straightened. Her face tightened. "You still blame my daughter for going to bed with Colin, don't you?"

"I can't help it."

"Why blame her? Have you ever thought of blaming Colin? For God's sake I went to bed with him, too. It may have been a brilliant script, Diana, but that little seduction didn't hurt his chances with me."

"That was before I knew him."

She stood. "I'm sorry I called you."

"Why did you, Ella?"

"I always thought you had your head screwed on right. Quite a feat in this town. I thought you'd understand that because I helped Colin you would now help me."

"That was a long time ago."

"Not to me. It seems like yesterday. My entire life seems like yesterday."

"You never had much interest in your daughter. Why now?"

"I can't see my reflection in her face." She walked into her bedroom and shut the door. I was left sitting in the eerily quiet pink-shaded room. Not even a clock ticked. I wondered if I would have helped Ella, no matter what I thought about Kera, if she were still Number One at the box office? After all I was a middle-aged actress who needed work. Unable to come up with an answer I walked down the grand staircase. No one applauded my exit.

That night I stood on my small rotting redwood deck facing the Pacific Ocean with a glass of red wine in my hand and the warm salty wind pulling gently at my hair. I was trying to figure out why I had never blamed Colin for going to bed with Kera Sands. At that time I had attempted the classic French shrug where Colin was concerned. *C'est la vie.* Except I'm American down to my toes and my shrug was as stiff as a puritan's soul and my French has always been mangled.

My gaze drifted from the ocean to the narrow walkway that separated my small house from Ryan Johns' multimillion-dollar enormous white blob of a mansion; it billowed up next to me like a giant illuminated marshmallow. Near the moonlit walkway I saw Ryan lying in a heap under his hibiscus bush. I balanced my wine on the railing, took the hose that curled in the corner, turned the water on full force, and sprayed him with it. Gasping for air he fought his way out of his stupor into a sitting position.

"Tidal wave! I'm drowning," he sputtered.

"You're drowning yourself in booze," I yelled back turning the hose off. "I thought I was doing a rewrite on the Titanic." He staggered to his feet. "I love it that you look after me, Diana."

Ryan was a big burly Irishman that looked like he was born in a pub, except he was born in Connecticut to a wealthy banking family that didn't understand their son's creativity. Or so he told me drunkenly over and over the night I mistakenly went out to dinner with him. His thick reddish-blond hair formed lovely ringlets when it was wet. They made me smile. He shook himself like a St. Barnard and almost fell over. Righting himself, he staggered up the steps to his veranda and announced:

"I just sold a script for five million today. I bet your husband never did that."

"Colin's dead Ryan. Why do you keep competing with him?"

"Nobody's dead to an Irishman." He collapsed on his chaise lounge and began to snore. I took my wine and went inside.

Sometime during the early morning hours of the next day Ella Sands fell down those dramatic stairs and broke her neck. I stood in my kitchen drinking coffee and watching Dr. Logan Bradford being interviewed on the morning TV news. Standing in front of Ella's palatial Beverly Hills white brick house he told the reporters that Ella might have had an aneurysm or a mild stroke causing her fall. Kera, his wife and Ella's daughter, he explained, was too distraught to talk to anybody. I studied Logan Bedford's face. He had sharp possessive eyes, the black hair of a gigolo, and pale antiseptic skin. I turned the TV off and wondered what Ella Sands was doing out of bed in the early morning hours. Maybe she hadn't been acting when I last talked to her. Maybe she really had been afraid for her life. And maybe if she had been Number One at the box office I would have offered my help. Maybe.

Four days later along with other mourners I was standing in Ella Sands' living room, dressed in my black suit, white pearls, and my wide-brimmed black straw hat. Show business people have a difficult time at funerals. We forget we're at a wake and immediately begin to talk about our next project, the script we're reading, and the money we're making. But we never talk about the money we're not making, or the script we're not reading, or the project we're not shooting. That would be too close to death.

Ryan Johns sidled up to me. His face was so sun burnt that the lines around his mouth and across his forehead showed white. He wore dark glasses.

"What happened to you?"

"You happened. You left me out on my veranda all night so I could fry in the morning sun. And this looks good. You should have seen me four days ago."

I laughed. "You're not my responsibility, Ryan."

His expression turned serious. "Yes, I am."

"Diana Poole?" A dark haired man with long delicate fingers

approached me. "I'm Doctor Logan Bradford. Kera's my wife."

"It's nice to meet you."

He took my hand in his cold grip. "I'm sorry it has to be under these circumstances."

"Where is Kera? I've been looking for her. I wanted to pay my respects."

"She's not able to come down. But she wondered if you could go up to her. She's in Ella's sitting room."

"Of course."

"Thank you." He moved quickly away as if he didn't want me to stare too long into his eyes.

Leaving Ryan, I went up the stairs and knocked on the sitting room door. A faint voice told me to come in. Kera sat in her mother's chair under her mother's portrait. Ella was right; I would not have recognized her. Her nose was small and perfect and therefore strangely unattractive in its careful blandness. Her cheeks had been implanted and raised, causing the bottom half of her face to appear longer than I had remembered. Her sharp, defiant chin so much like her mother's had been softened. There were no lines, no life in her face. She didn't look like she had come from the passion of a man and a woman. She looked as if she'd been wrought from her husband's cold fingers. Her thick auburn hair had been dyed a heavy black.

"Do you know I don't even know who my father is? " she said, simply. "Mother wasn't sure. Growing up I hoped he was James Dean and it was because he had died so young that I had never heard from him." She smiled an unfamiliar smile. "It's been a long time. How are you?"

"Fine." I sat down in the same chair I had sat in earlier that week.

"I hear you're acting again," she said.

"I need the money and it's the only thing I know how to do."

"You're lucky you know how to do something. I never bothered to learn. I know you're here for mother and not me. I suppose everyone downstairs is here for her and not me," she said resentfully. "Did you meet Logan?"

"Briefly. Kera I want to talk to you about a conversation I had with your mother."

"Did Logan come upstairs with you?" Nervously twisting a laced-edged handkerchief with hands that looked much older than her face, she peered at the sitting room door.

"No, I came alone."

"I thought I heard something. Would you check for me, see if he's in the hallway?"

I opened the door and found Ryan on his knees listening at the keyhole.

"What are you doing?" I asked in a low voice.

He clasped hands together. "Will you marry me?"

Who is it?" Kera asked anxiously.

"It's just Ryan. He's drunk."

"I am not," he mouthed, indignantly.

I closed the door on him. "Why did you think it was your husband?"

"Mother's death has put me on edge." Pulling at the hem of her black dress she shifted uneasily in her chair. "Did you know Mother adored Ryan Johns? She had an affair with him. I think she had a soft spot for writers. I had an affair with him, too. It was around the time ..." she stopped.

"That I found you in bed with my husband? Maybe like your mother you also have a soft spot for writers."

"I think you're still angry at me, Diana."

"After ten years the word angry is a little extreme."

"Why do we always blame the woman and never the man?" Her strangely tilted eyes met mine. I could still see her mother's familiar glint in them.

"Your mother asked me the same question."

"Do you remember when we were young, maybe nineteen, driving down Sunset Boulevard? And you pointed out all the houses that you liked, trying to decide which one you would live in when you were a rich movie star. I never pointed out one because I lived in a movie star's house. And now it is mine. And Logan's," she added ruefully.

"Kera, before your mother died she told me she was worried about you."

"Are you sure you have the right mother?" She forced a laugh, a pale copy of Ella's deep sexual laugh.

"Ella wanted me to contact you, to see if you were happy in your marriage."

"Mother and I were like star-crossed lovers always communicating through liaisons. Always misinterpreting one another. I am going to miss her, Diana." Tears slowly dropped one by one down her creaseless face. She was like a statue crying.

"She was also worried about herself," I persisted.

"When wasn't she?" She dabbed at her cheeks.

"Kera, she thought that your husband wanted to kill her."

She bit at her lower lip, then asked, "Did you believe her?"

"No. But now that she ..."

"Fell down the stairs? Diana, I've always lacked confidence. Mother thought my lack of confidence was a weapon, something I contrived, just to get back at her, to make her feel inept because I was a failure. She didn't like Logan because he gave me confidence. He did a few things to my face that made me feel better about myself. That's all." Her voice was shrill and defensive.

"I just thought you should hear what she told me."

She stared into her lap. When she looked at me there was fear in her eyes. "He keeps finding things wrong with me. He tells me I need this done, that done." She grabbed my hand. "I know what I look like. Oh, God, he has a mistress and ..."

The door opened and Logan Bradford came in. "Are you ladies having a nice chat?" His long meticulously kept fingers smoothed his slick hair. I didn't like the way he said the word 'ladies'.

"Yes we are, Logan," Kera said, submissively.

He looked up at Ella's portrait. "I think we should hang that downstairs in the living room. What do you think, Kera?"

"Whatever you want, Logan."

"Really?" He stared at her with contempt. "Then what I want is for you to rest."

"Do you mind, Diana? I am tired."

"Not at all."

Outside on the lawn under the liquid amber trees the mourners peering from behind their sunglasses conversed in somber groups. Near the portable bar I saw Ryan talking to a young actress. He was writing something down on a piece of paper. She was swaying her body against his while she flipped her long golden hair back from her creaseless face.

"I want to talk to you," I said, joining them.

"Diana, you have such a gentle way about you. This is Sydney spelled with 'i'. I haven't quite figured out just where the 'i' is placed."

"Anywhere you want," she cooed and swayed away.

"Her phone number." He waved it under my nose then put it in his pocket.

"Why were you listening at the door?"

"I wanted to hear what Kera had to say about her mother."

"Why?"

He pushed his glasses down to the tip of his crooked pugilistic nose and stared at me with intelligent, mischievous, red-rimmed eyes.

"I loved Ella. When I was a very young lad and new in town I met her at a party. She took me home and into her bed. I couldn't believe it. The first woman I bedded in Hollywood was Ella Sands. I still can't believe it."

"I hear she went to bed with most men."

"But only one at a time," he countered. "I felt very special. The next morning I saw Kera sitting out by that pool." He gestured with his drink to an Olympic-size pool shimmering baby blue in the relentless sunlight. "She stared at me as if I were – well, what I was – just another man coming into her mother's bed for the night then tip toeing out in the morning. But it was a look I'll never forget. One of true hatred. But I understood it. I felt sorry for her."

"Kera told me you had an affair with her, too."

"But much later. She was like trying to make love to a shadow."

"Her mother's?"

"Yes. What do you think of Logan Bedford? "

"He's a domineering snake."

"I love the way women talk. Images slightly askew, but the meaning so clear."

"Ella told me that Bedford wanted to kill her."

His eyebrows arched over his sunglasses. "Are you saying she didn't fall down the stairs?"

"I don't know what I'm saying. You can go back to Sydney with an 'i', wherever it is. I'm going home."

"I'll go with you."

"Where's your car?"

"They took my license away. I had to take a cab here." He guided me across the lawn. "The driver couldn't find Beverly Hills. And I only know how to get around this town when I'm drunk. So we got lost in a town called Mar Vista, where you cannot see the ocean from any point. Why are words never what they mean in this world of ours, Diana?" he asked, forlornly.

"You mean like the word love?" I asked. Again I felt the pain of loss.

With the sun in our eyes and the palm trees swaying in the warm breeze like melancholy hula dancers, Ryan and I waited in the driveway for the valet to bring my car around. Logan Bradford stepped out of the house.

"May I speak to you for a moment? Alone." He took my arm and guided me away from Ryan. Leaning close he asked, "What did my wife tell you?"

"I don't know what you mean?"

"What did she say about me?"

"We talked about Ella."

"She hated her mother. She wouldn't spend time talking about her. What did she tell you?" He pressed his steel-like fingers into my arm.

"Let go of me."

"Whatever she said to you is a lie."

Ryan stepped between us. "Your car is here, Diana," he announced, preemptively.

In the car Ryan asked, "What did the domineering snake want?"

"He wanted to know what Kera and I were talking about. He thought it was about him."

"I hear he has chiseled her into *his* version of a woman. Except I also hear he doesn't like women."

"He likes us well enough to be having an affair with one. Kera looks terrible." I turned left onto Sunset Boulevard and flipped the visor down. I drove past some of the same mansions that years ago Kera and I had driven by. I tried to remember which ones I had chosen to live in when I was going be rich and famous. But I couldn't.

"Why did she let him do it to her? " Ryan asked.

"She's afraid of him."

"Could we turn the air conditioning on?"

"It doesn't work."

"Why do you cling to this old Jag?"

"Because I can't afford a new car."

"Let me buy you one, then you can drive me around town and I won't get lost in Mar Vista where you can't see the ocean."

"Ryan, why did you go to bed with Kera?"

"I'll go to bed with anybody. I also thought in my infinite self-centeredness that I could keep her from seducing your husband."

"You must not have been very good."

"I'll have you know that I performed like a stallion. Well, maybe a very lusty Shetland pony. If you remember, you and Colin had separated over some stupid argument."

"I don't even remember what it was. I don't even remember what great mansion I wanted to live in when I was nineteen."

"Mansion? You're not desperate enough to live in a mansion. What are you talking about?"

"Time." As I curved further west on Sunset I could feel those big houses and my youth receding from me like ocean waves that lap at your ankles and then swiftly pull away.

"I'll tell you why you and Colin were arguing," Ryan said. "It was two creative temperamental egos colliding. If you hadn't decided to makeup with Colin and then come back to the house in the middle of the night to surprise him, you wouldn't have found him with Kera. What I mean is, he would never have gone to bed with her if he knew you had wanted to come back. Why do women always want to surprise men anyway? I think you unconsciously want to catch us at our worst."

"Maybe we want to catch you at your best."

"If that's the case then Colin, the great man of taste and discretion, failed, didn't he?"

I looked sharply at Ryan. He was grinning, pleased at the thought of a discredited Colin. Too pleased.

We stopped at the light where Sunset Boulevard ends and the Pacific Ocean begins. The waves splashed on sand so smooth and flat that it looked like a cheap beige carpet.

Late that night the doorbell rang, jarring me awake. I peered at the clock. It was eleven-thirty. Out of habit I looked at the other half of the bed for help. It was empty; Colin's pillow firmed and plumped. Untouched. I got up and threw on my robe and padded across the cool Mexican pavers into the hallway. Peering through the peephole I saw Kera's waxen face illuminated by the porch light. Fear pulled at her lips and eyes, distorting her into grotesqueness. I opened the door.

"This is the only place I could think of where Logan wouldn't know to find me." Half dazed, she wandered into the living room. "I'll leave if you want me to."

"Don't be silly. I'll get you a drink."

When I came back with a brandy, she was standing out on the balcony staring at the ocean. Her hand shook when she took the glass.

"What happened?" I asked.

"The night mother died Logan wasn't at home with me. I thought he was with his mistress. This evening I confronted him about what mother had told you and he went into a rage. I'm afraid of him. Can I stay here just 'til morning?"

"Well, I ..."

"Please, Diana."

"I'll put you up on the sofa."

"Who's that?" She pulled a gun from her coat pocket and aimed toward the walkway and the swaying hibiscus bush.

"Don't turn the bloody hose on me," Ryan roared, staggering to his feet.

"It's Ryan Johns. He's drunk," I told her.

"Will somebody help me with him?" a woman whined. Golden Sydney with an 'i' came into the light of my deck. "This is the worst evening of my life." Her eyes came to rest on the gun quivering in Kera's hand.

"Hello, Sydni," Kera greeted coldly.

"Kera?" Sydni froze.

"*You* had an awful evening," Ryan suddenly bellowed at the young actress then began to make his case to us. "I had to spend it talking to a viped vaper. Vapid viper. Flipping her hair, clicking her nails, licking her lips. She even flossed."

"I was bored," Sydni snapped at him, forgetting the gun in Kera's hand. "I went out with you because you said you had a part for me in your new script. And all you did was talk about your parents not understanding you. I thought you got over that when you're middle-aged."

"Middle *what*?"

Sydni turned on Kera. "And if you're trying to scare me with that gun it won't work."

"*Gun*?' Ryan tired to focus.

"Did you think it wasn't proper to see my husband on the night of mother's funeral?' Kera asked her.

"Logan thought he should be with you and not me tonight."

"Jesus, it is a gun," Ryan said. "Why do you have a gun?" He lurched toward my stair rail and bumped into Sydni. "Oh, Christ, the vipid vaper is still here."

Kera slipped the gun back into her pocket and walked into my house.

Now Sydni ranted at me. "He slobbered all over me, never once mentioned his new script, and then looked at his watch, leaped up, and said we have to leave. And tell that bitch if she's trying to scare Logan and me it won't work." She turned on Ryan. "God, you're disgusting." She stalked back down the narrow passage toward Pacific Coast Highway and her car.

"Am I disgusting, Diana?" he asked, like a little boy.

"Yes."

"Why does Kera have a gun?"

"She's afraid of Bedford."

"I am disgusting."

"Go to bed."

I went into the living room and closed the sliding glass doors and locked them. Kera sat on the sofa. Her hair was dead black against her eerily pale skin. Exhausted I sat down across from her.

"How long has your husband been seeing Sydni?" I asked.

"About three months. She's perfect."

"She's young."

"He hasn't done a thing to her. I want you to know, Diana, that I didn't go to bed with your husband to take him away from you."

"You couldn't have done that even if you had wanted to."

"I went to bed with him because mother had gone to bed with him. When I was old enough I made a pact with myself. I would seduce every one of mother's lovers. And it would be my secret until it was the right time to tell her, until it would wound her deeply. But I never found the right time," she added, desolately.

I stared at Colin's two Oscars on the mantel. Casting their twin shadows on the wall they glimmered with sleek pride.

"What did Colin say to you when you went to bed with him?" I asked.

"Why do you want to know what he said?"

"He cared about words."

"Who can remember? I didn't mean anything to Colin."

"He wouldn't have gone to bed with you if you'd meant nothing to him. What did he say?"

I had never asked Colin for an explanation and he had never offered one.

"We had great sex that was all. It was nothing."

Only in Hollywood can great sex equal nothing, I thought. Again I could see her mother's eyes glinting out at me and I knew she was lying. I knew it had meant something.

"I'll take the gun." I held out my hand. She hesitated then reached into her pocket and handed it to me. "Who was this for?"

"Me. Maybe Logan. I'm tired of being hurt. Of being second best."

I made a bed for her on the sofa then I went back to my room. But I couldn't sleep, not with a woman I didn't trust on my sofa and her loaded gun on my nightstand. At two o'clock the doorbell rang. I peered at Colin's pillow. Then wrapping my robe around me, I hurried out to the foyer. Kera was already there.

"It's Logan," she said, frantically.

I looked out the peephole. "I don't see anybody."

"He must've gone around to the ocean side of the house. Where's the gun?"

"You don't need it." We went into the living room. Logan Bedford appeared on my deck and began pounding hard on the sliding glass door. The glass shook in its frame. I unlocked the door and slid it open about an inch.

"She doesn't want to see you. Go away or I'll call the police."

He shoved the door wide and pushed me out of the way with such force I slammed against the wall, striking my head. Kera screamed and rushed toward my bedroom. Bedford strode down the hall after her. Dazed I leaned on the back of a chair.

"No more. No more, Kera," he yelled from my room. Then there was the sound of a slap. Kera whimpered. The gun went off. I staggered into the bedroom. The smell of nitrite and the intimate smell of my own perfume mixed with the salt air. I leaned against the door jam. Logan Bedford was sprawled on his back on the bed, his head on Colin's pillow. Blood spread across his chest and seeped from his open mouth onto my sheets. Kera stood at the foot of the bed, the gun still in her hand. She slowly lifted it to her head. I lurched for her and grabbed it. Collapsing in a chair, she covered her expressionless face with her aging hands.

Three hours later I stood on Ryan's veranda pounding on his French doors. Since my bedroom was a murder scene I had no place else to go. Yellow tape had been draped around my small house. The lights were still on and the police were still there. I had told them everything that had happened. Kera had called her lawyer who had come to the house. She was allowed to leave in his custody. The French doors finally opened.

"Am I dreaming?" Ryan muttered.

"I need to stay here for the night. Or what's left of it. Kera shot the good doctor in my bedroom."

"Kera did? Are you all right?"

"Didn't you hear the commotion?"

"I sleep deeply when I'm passed out. But if I'd been awake and sober I would have rescued you." He guided me into his overly decorated living room.

"Forget it. I'm too old to be rescued." I sank into a sofa that was obese with down feathers and watched Ryan as he fixed us drinks. He didn't look like a man who had been asleep.

Two days later Ryan and I stood in my bedroom staring at my new Beautyrest mattress. The other one had been soaked with Dr. Logan Bedford's blood.

"The least Kera could have done is pay for it," he said. "Would you like to christen it?" He wiggled his eyebrows at me.

"No."

"Inaugurate it?"

"No."

"Diana, it's no longer Colin's bed."

"Is that why I feel so betrayed?"

Grabbing me he pressed my body to his and awkwardly kissed me. I stepped back from his embrace. Flushed, he managed an expression of bemusement, but his blue eyes shone with rejection.

"I'm sorry, Ryan. But I keep thinking about the night Kera shot her husband. Seeing him lying on my bed. I feel as if I've somehow been taken advantage of. As if I had been in a play. And everybody was acting their roles except me because I didn't know the script."

"Forget it. You had an out-of-body experience. It happens when you're witnessing something horrifying. I felt it just now when you couldn't wait to get away from me."

"Ryan, why did you go out with Sydni that night? "

"Why not? "

"It just seems odd that Sydni should show up here exactly when Kera did. And what about the police cars, the ambulance? You had to hear the sirens."

"I have rewrites to do and a bottle of Scotch to finish."

"Ryan, answer me."

"I felt sorry for Kera. Somebody has to feel sorry for the shadows of our world."

"I don't understand."

"Kera wanted me to bring Sydni back to my house at the same time she would be waiting on the deck of your house."

"Because she knew that Syndi would call Bedford and tell him where she was?"

"I didn't know he would be shot. But he did kill her mother and mutilate her."

"Did he?"

"Leave it be, Diana. Like Colin I just felt sorry for her."

"Are you saying Colin went to bed with Kera because he felt sorry for her?"

"Thanks for not wiping my kiss off with the back of your hand, Diana."

He left me staring at my bare pristine mattress. My feeling of betrayal turned to anger. I grabbed my keys and purse and drove to Beverly Hills.

The sun was going down, casting the white brick house into pink shadows. I knocked on the front door, but no one answered. I walked around to the back. The liquid-amber trees were turning black in the dimming light. I stepped in through an open den door, walked into the hallway, and up the curved stairs. Kera, with her back to me, was in the sitting room staring up at her mother's portrait: the young Ella Sands peered down at her grown daughter with that same perplexed expression. When I closed the door behind me Kera turned quickly around.

"Diana? You have the same look on your face that you had when you found me in bed with Colin."

I leaned against the door. "You set me up. I was the perfect witness, wasn't I? Someone who doesn't like you, who wouldn't lie for you."

She tossed her dead-black hair back from her face. "My mother unintentionally set you up. She told me she had talked to you. She told me she thought Logan wanted to harm us. She had it all wrong as usual. But that's because she never paid any attention to me." Self-pity pulled at her lips.

"So you shoved her down the stairs."

"I told her about how I had gone to bed with each one of her lovers. She didn't want to hear it. She ran out into the hallway. I couldn't stand the expression on her face. Her self-hatred."

"Or was it your own self-hatred you couldn't stand? Did Ryan know you killed her?"

"No. Nor did he know I intended to kill Logan. I just got him to take out Sydni."

"But why kill your husband?"

"Logan was fine as long as he did exactly what I wanted, which was to erase mother's likeness from my face. His reward was marrying into a small fortune and keeping his mistress. But he guessed I had killed mother. Funny, he was afraid that I was going to tell people that he did it."

"One more question. What really happened between you and Colin besides great sex?" I added, sarcastically.

"I already told you."

"No, you were lying. I could see it in your eyes. You know I can still see your mother in your eyes?"

Kera stiffened.

"And look at your hands. They look exactly like your mother's."

She peered down at her hands, clenching them and unclenching them.

"Haven't you heard, Kera? We all end up looking like our mothers. Did you really think you would be the only one who didn't? "

"That's not true. It's not true! And your Colin was a big failure in bed. He just wanted to put his arms around me and hold me." Resentment narrowed her eyes. "I've never wanted to get out of a man's bed so fast in my entire life. God, I was glad when you showed up." Again she attempted her mother's worldly laugh and failed.

"Oh, Kera, you should have let him comfort you."

It was dark when I returned to Malibu. I poured a glass of wine and went outside and breathed in the ocean air and tried to remember the touch of my husband's embrace. In the walkway the hibiscus bush shook. I peered down at the heap that was Ryan Johns. In his stupor he muttered and kicked his feet as if he were running away from something. Everybody is running away in this town, trying to get out from under the shadow of the more famous, the more wealthy, the more creative, the more loved, the more beautiful. And most of them don't make it, yet they never think of leaving. They stay silhouetted against those they hate, envy, or can never have. I left Ryan and went back into the house and lay down on my bare Beautyrest mattress. I knew I had to call the police. Let them try to capture all the shadows. I reached for my husband's pillow but it wasn't there.

A woman I know confessed to me that she found a Tiffany box in the snow one evening in front of the famous jewelry store. Picking it up and moving further down the sidewalk, she opened it and discovered a pair of earrings. She kept them. But her guilt would never let her wear them. The moral? Never confess your sins to a writer.

TIFFANY BLUE

"How can James do this to me, Diana?" Julie Plume asked, as we walked past Tiffany's. It was five o'clock on a cold wintry day, and Fifth Avenue was beginning to fill with office-workers hurrying for home or the nearest bar.

"The movie's wrapped and he's gone back to his wife," I explained.

Was it her youth or the insularity of her beauty that kept Julie from grasping the more simple facts of life? Or was I just too old and too jaded? I gave her a sideways glance. She was wearing a black hat pulled low over her natural blonde hair. My hair was determinedly blonde. A red muffler nestled her firm defiant chin. My chin was softening. Her turned-up nose and high cheekbones were flush from the cold, making her look even younger and shockingly wholesome. I don't think I ever looked wholesome, even when I was. Her black coat was pulled tightly around her lithe supple figure. My feet were killing me. Yes, I was too old and too jaded.

"I hate it when filming ends, Diana. I feel like I've been abandoned, like I've been left by my parents or something. I should have realized when we were in bed and I whispered in his ear, 'Jimmy, Jimmy,' and he told me to call him James that our affaire wasn't going anywhere."

I laughed. "Maybe the name Jimmy makes him feel like a little boy."

"He told me that only his wife calls him Jimmy."

I remembered the feel of his wife's quivering hand in mine when I had first met her. It was a more vivid memory than the feel of James' body on my body, or his lips on my lips. In fact, I couldn't remember his intimate touch at all. Only his wife's small nervous hand. It was like grasping a sparrow. How many years ago was that? Twenty? Or more?

"Why did you go to bed with him in the first place?" I asked, pulling up the collar of my camel-colored coat. "You know his reputation. He always goes back to Carol."

I marveled at how I could ask her this without feeling hypocritical. Time, and a husband whom I loved deeply until his death, had intervened. My brief affaire with James Barron no longer mattered in my life. Except that I had just finished acting in his new movie. But that's, as they say, *show biz*.

"He's a brilliant director. The most important one I've worked with, that's why I went to bed with him."

"You've only worked with one other director, Julie."

"James brought something out in me I didn't know I had. You saw it in the dailies. Everybody saw it. They're talking *Oscar*, Diana." Her green eyes flashed with triumph.

Unbelievably, they *were* talking Oscar performance. Julie and I had just come from viewing the dailies. Sitting in the darkness of the screening room I had marveled at how the camera loved her beauty, but also how it had magnified her extraordinary lack of depth and emotion. James had corrected for her lack of talent by allowing her to say only five or six words in a scene; then he'd quickly cut to me, or one of the other lesser-known actors. By not letting his camera linger on Julie, he had created mystery where there was none. And isn't that what good filmmaking is all about? Yet sitting there in the dark I knew the movie wasn't any good. I knew that James Barron had lost his touch.

"I thought James and I had developed something," Julie continued. "You know, like Woody Allen and Diane Keaton. Or even Mia Farrow. It's not like I expected our relationship to last forever, but just long enough for him to star me in two or three of his films. I know he's not as hot as he used to be, but I thought he could put me over the top. You know what he's going to do next?"

"What?"

"Some script about two men and an elephant. The only woman in it is a middle-aged zoologist. Can you believe it?" she asked, appalled.

Middle-aged? I made a mental note of this since parts for women my age did not come along that often. "What's the title of the script?" I asked, nonchalantly.

Ignoring my question she stopped and stared bleakly into a dirty gray snow bank. People swerved around us unaware that it was the soon-to-be-famous Julie Plume and the vaguely familiar but not-in-the-least-bit-famous Diana Poole who were blocking their way.

"I can't believe James is dumping me." Her eyes shined with a disquieting intensity.

"Did you honestly think you would be different? So this new script is about two men and a zoologist?" I tried not to sound too desperate.

"Elephant. Why does he always go back to his wife? I mean, don't you find that weird?"

"Maybe he loves Carol. Do you know the title of the script or not?" The direct approach was always better with Julie.

"Are you being serious?" she demanded.

"About what?"

"About James loving Carol? I can't believe how naïve you are, and at *your* age."

I smiled. "My age allows me to be serious about many things, even love. And it is a serious business, Julie. I'd be careful if I were you. Can we walk? I'm getting cold. I want to get back to the hotel."

But she stayed rooted to the middle of the sidewalk. "What if I can't act without him?" she asked.

"Don't be silly. You're on your way to being a huge star. Don't dissipate your energies. It can all be lost so easily. And be gracious to Carol tonight." I was very gracious to her twenty-some years ago, I thought guiltily.

"He invited *his wife* to his wrap party?" Her eyes widened incredulously.

"He always does. She flew in from L.A. this morning."

"Well that's a slap in the face, isn't it?"

"Whose face are we talking about?"

"Look!" She said in a low intense voice.

I followed her gaze. Nestled in the dirty gray snow bank, and briefly caught in the lights of a cab pulling away from the curb, was a little blue box tied with a white ribbon. Julie picked it up.

"It's from Tiffany's." She spoke in quiet awe as if she had just entered St. Patrick's Cathedral.

"Someone getting into that cab must've dropped it." I stared down Fifth Avenue at a mass of red taillights. Exhaust curled up from the cars and undulated on their yellow trunks like beckoning apparitions.

"It's small. That means jewelry." Julie's breath made a ghostly curl upward toward the blackening sky. She held the box to her ear as if she had discovered a seashell in the snow then shook it. "It's jewelry," she confirmed.

"Give it to the store's doorman. He'll take care of it." I looked back at Tiffany's; its windows glowed like giant candelabras flickering seductively in a rich dark room.

"The doorman? Are you kidding? He'll just give it to his wife, or girlfriend, or try to sell it." She slipped the little blue box into her coat pocket and walked quickly away. She was putting as much distance between herself and Tiffany's as fast as she could.

"What are you doing?" I asked, trying to keep up with her.

"I want to see what's in it." Maintaining her fast pace she took off her glove and slipped her bare hand inside her coat pocket. After a few moments she announced. "I have the ribbon off. And now the lid. I feel something cold and wonderful."

She removed her hand from her pocket. Resting in her palm was a diamond and emerald earring in the shape of a large shimmering teardrop. She quickly thrust her hand back into her pocket. "Is that not the most beautiful thing you've ever seen, Diana? And to think, they come in pairs like socks."

Her march was stopped by a red light. Cars filled the intersection. Pedestrians milled.

Catching my breath I managed to say, "We can give the earrings to a salesperson if you don't trust the doorman."

"How do we know a salesperson won't keep the earrings?" She was whispering now, aware of the people waiting impatiently around us. "There's no sales slip or anything."

"Well you can't keep them. Someone will be back looking for them."

"Lower your voice. Let me think about this."

"What do you have to think about?" I whispered. "Someone bought those for a gift. Maybe he wanted to give them to her tonight."

"*Gift? He? Her?* My, my, aren't you the romantic," she observed, sarcastically.

When did romance and love become so disdainful to the young? I wondered. I must've been in love with my husband and not noticed the change.

"Is that why you went to bed with James?" she asked in a low insinuating voice.

I was taken aback. How did she know? Did he tell her?

"Look, I was younger than you and it was my first acting role, and his first chance at directing. We were both scared. We helped each other get through it." Ah, revision. Or the truth? I wasn't sure anymore.

"Oh, I see, you were doing a good deed. Was he married to Carol then?"

But Carol's hand did tremble in mine. "What does any of this have to do with you stealing earrings?"

"There's stealing and there's stealing. That's all," she said, blithely.

"I'm not going to stand on this freezing cold corner and discuss moral equivalency with you."

Julie looked thoughtful. "You know, I don't think there is any romance connected to these earrings. I think some old wealthy woman with saggy ear lobes bought these for herself. Someone who has nothing better to do with her time or money. A woman like James' wife."

"The woman could be Ivana Trump for all I care. The earrings do not belong to you."

"Keep your voice down. Oh, I see. Nothing belongs to me. Not James. Not the earrings. I wonder what belongs to Carol? Did you ever ask yourself that, Diana?" She suddenly laughed and put her arm around mine as if we were the best of friends. Her cheeks and nose were red like a kid's.

"I promise I'll return the earrings tomorrow. I just want to wear them tonight to James' party. I've never had anything so beautiful. I feel like Cinderella."

The light changed. As Julie dashed across the street she flashed her heartbreakingly beautiful smile at me as if I was her fairy godmother and she was thanking me for a magical act I had just accomplished. But I was no fairy godmother. I was an actress who understood the rules of the game. And Julie? Well, I don't know what she understood.

James Barron's party was being held in a private dining room in the hotel where 'the talent', as the production people liked to refer to us, were staying. The party was in full swing when I arrived. French mirrored walls reflected crystal chandeliers. Candlelight glowed on black silk-covered tables. The actors, the upper echelon of the crew, and the various producers and moneymen formed little groups where they talked, lied, and laughed. Julie stood in the middle of the room wearing a lime-green slip of a gown and pretending to hang on every word of her leading man, the moody Lucas Caine. The diamond and emerald teardrops, dangling from her delicate lobes, erupted in small bursts of light like a Lilliputian Fourth of July.

"Diana, you look wonderful." Howard Marsh threw his arms around me and swayed me back and forth in one of his great bear hugs. Then with a quaint swashbuckling elegance he swept two glasses of champagne from the tray of a passing waiter, handed me one, and bowed. Then he looked forlornly around the room.

"We're out of work again, darling." He heaved a theatrical sigh.

"Waiting for the phone to ring again, darling." I imitated his sigh and smoothed my burgundy velvet suit jacket.

"There's something regressive about waiting for the phone to ring. It's not as if we're actors at all, but just a group of desperate old pimply-faced teenagers still waiting to be asked out. Cheers."

After we clinked our glasses and drank I casually asked, "Did you hear about James' next project?"

"Something about two men and a Rhino."

"A zoologist. What's it called?"

"I have no idea. I know there's nothing in it for me. All the male parts will be for twenty year olds. I wonder how old the Rhino is? Did you see those earrings Julie is wearing?"

I nodded as Julie tossed her head back and laughed at something Lucas said. Since he had no sense of humor and she couldn't act, her laughter sounded loud and forced as if she had been practicing it alone in front of her mirror. I knew this display of mirth was for James' benefit. Seemingly oblivious of her he lurked in a dim corner. In his late forties, and wearing small dark glasses and a black suit, James Barron looked as if he were attending a funeral instead of hosting his own party. He was also dyeing his hair, a sign that he was afraid of losing that all-important audience: the young. The pressures of Hollywood have so little to do with talent. Next to him was Marcus, his cinematographer, a tall distant man who was listing from too many Martinis.

"I know Julie has no conscience," Howard sniffed. "But I can't believe she has the guts to wear those earrings."

"I see she told you what happened. Of course she has the guts."

"She shouldn't be blabbing it around."

"She promised she'd return ..."

"Ixnay. The Tantrum is approaching with The Wife," he warned under his breath. The Tantrum was Howard's name for one of our eight producers, a man who had all the emotional restraint of an infant.

"My two favorite actors," he greeted us. Any actor he was talking to was his favorite, but Howard and I immediately forgot this and beamed gratefully under his compliment.

The Tantrum tilted his fetus-shaped head toward his companion and said, "You both know Carol Barron, James' wife?"

"Of course we know Carol," we gushed in unison, and too eagerly. Then I felt her hand in mine. Her fingers no longer trembled. It was just another lifeless handshake.

"I haven't seen you in ages, Diana." She was proudly thin, as if that was where she had placed all her energies. Her dark hair was cut into a short severe style; it looked like a protective helmet. "I hear you're very good in the film."

"The real surprise of the movie is Julie Plume," The Tantrum announced with his usual insensitivity.

Carol forced a thin-lipped smile. "Yes, I hear she's great. James knows how to get the best out of his actresses."

Her tired brown eyes met my tired blue ones and I knew she knew. But was it about Julie? Or me? Or all the other actresses who had a quick affaire with her husband, and then left discreetly, so he could return to her?

"Are those earrings real?" The Tantrum's puffy eyes were riveted on Julie. His moist baby-mouth hung open.

"Of course they're real," Carol answered. "My husband always tries for reality. Excuse me." She eased away from us.

"What did she mean by that?" I asked.

"I thought you knew. James gave Julie those earrings," Howard said, shaking his head in dismay.

"What?"

"He better not have charged the production for them," The Tantrum grumbled. Forgetting that Howard and I existed, he turned his back on us and began to talk to one of his co-producers.

"Howard," I said. "James didn't buy Julie those earrings. She found them in a snow bank."

He blessed me with his fatherly smile. Howard had the paternal look down perfectly. He'd been playing Julie's father in the movie.

"Don't tell me you believe her story, Diana? She actually winked at me when she told it."

Before I could respond, Lucas Caine sidled up to me and slipped his arm around my waist. "I wish I was man enough to go to bed with an older woman. But I know you'd make me feel ineffectual."

"God, what a line you have, Lucas." Howard rolled his eyes.

"That line gets me out of more problems." A lock of Lucas' hair, the color of chocolate cake, flopped onto his forehead. Irritated that there was a part of his body he couldn't control, he huffily pushed the errant strand back into its proper place then glanced over at Julie. She was now talking to one of the movie's five screenwriters.

"How could James give her those earrings when he only gave me a travel clock from Tiffany's?" he demanded. "I worked my ass off making her look good. And who uses travel clocks anymore?"

"If he spent that much money maybe he really loves her," Howard observed.

"*Love?*" Lucas repeated the word as if he had never heard it before.

"Well, it's the only answer I can come up with." Howard blushed, embarrassed at his own sentimentality. Why were people my age suddenly self-conscious about love?

"As far I know he's never given any of his other conquests a gift like that," he added defensively.

"James did not give her those earrings," I said. "She found them in a snow bank."

"Diana, you're a woman of the world. How can you believe a stupid story like that?" Lucas asked, letting his eyes follow the strand of pearls that curved around my neck and down into my cleavage.

"Because I was with her."

But he wasn't listening. His eyes had darted quickly away from my cleavage, and he was now talking to Howard. "James owes Julie. Big time. He bought her off because she won't play the game, so she won't tell The Wife. But he wasted his money. The wife knows. Everyone knows."

"Everyone always knows," Howard said, sagely.

Diana The Undaunted tried again. "I was with Julie. We were walking down Fifth Avenue. She saw a little blue box with a white ribbon tied around it in a snow bank ..."

"Sure, Diana. She found the earrings all tied up in a Tiffany box." Again Lucas slid his arm around my waist and drew me to him. "Would you really make me feel ineffectual?"

"Yes. Excuse me."

I made my way across the room to Julie. She was standing at the buffet table with an empty plate in her hand staring down at the lush display of lobster, cracked crab, oysters, clams, and shrimp.

"Can I eat any of this?" she asked me. "I'm on a macramé diet."

"Macrobiotic. Come here, I want to talk with you."

"You're hurting my arm," she said, as I firmly guided her over to a secluded corner filled by a desolate looking palm. Hotels must grow these plants in their basements, I thought.

"You better not have bruised me, Diana. I'm suppose to have pictures taken for Vogue tomorrow," she whined inspecting her arm.

"Did you tell everyone that James gave you those earrings?" I demanded.

"No. I told them the truth."

"So why do they all think he gave them to you?"

"We live in cynical times. I can't help it if people choose not to believe the truth. Isn't lobster high in cholesterol?" She looked longingly back at the buffet.

"You don't have cholesterol. I don't think you even have a pulse. Howard said you winked at him when you told him about finding the Tiffany box. A wink can undercut the truth, Julie. And you're just the kind of actress who'd try such an obvious gesture."

Anger pulled the corners of her mouth down. "Remember, Diana, they're talking Oscar. And Howard always thinks I'm winking at him."

"You want everyone to believe James gave you those earrings. That's why you wanted to keep them, isn't it? Cinderella, my ass."

"God, I didn't realize how jealous you are of James and me."

"I'm not thinking of you two, I'm thinking of The Wife."

"Did you think about The Wife when you went to bed with him? I told everybody the truth. My conscience is clear."

"Be careful, Julie. A wife has a tendency to draw the line when she thinks her husband is giving expensive jewelry from to his girlfriend."

"What's the worst she can do? Leave him?" She asked with feigned innocence.

"You can't really want him."

"He understands my abilities as an actress." She displayed her perfect smile then turned on her heels, blonde hair fanning out, and returned to the buffet. I took a long swallow of warm champagne.

"I've been trying to remember the first time we met." Carol Barron approached. "It was James' first movie, wasn't it?"

"Yes."

"A long time ago."

"A long time ago."

"We met on the set. Do you remember?"

"Yes."

"We've both changed a great deal since then."

"Yes."

"I'm sorry about your husband."

"Thank you. I never thought I'd go back to acting but I have to pay the bills now," I chatted uneasily.

Carol peered at Julie who, still holding an empty plate, was talking to The Tantrum.

"Did James ever give you anything as beautiful as those earrings?" she asked.

"Why should he?" I stammered, and then quickly added, "James didn't give those to her. She found them in a snow bank near Tiffany's."

Deep lines curved around her wry smile. "You must think I'm some poor desperate woman who has no self respect. And maybe I am. But don't insult my intelligence, it's all I have left."

"I know it sounds implausible, but I was with Julie when she found them. She's just wearing them for tonight. Like Cinderella." *Oh, God.* "She's going to return them tomorrow."

"Cinderella?" She laughed harshly. "Julie's just another bad actress in another of James' bad movies. Do you remember when he made good movies?"

"Yes."

"I loved him then."

I knew she was saying she loved him when I had had an affaire with him. We smiled at each other and sipped our champagne.

"How can I convince you that Julie's story is true?" I asked. "If you can't believe her then at least believe me. I was with her."

"Why should I believe you?" she asked evenly.

"Because ..." I stopped. She was right. Why should she believe me? And why did I want her to?

"Are you trying to correct a wrong, Diana?"

"No. Maybe. Look, I do know the truth abut the earrings. That's all."

"Only I can correct what is wrong. Let's talk about something else. Do you know you'd be perfect for the role of the zoologist in James' next movie?"

"Really? What's it called?" I marveled at how I could still play the game even while I was trying to ease my own guilt. I was too old and too jaded. And God knows my feet still hurt.

"I don't know the title. Something about two men and a Giraffe. I'm tired. Will you tell James I've gone up to our room?" Carol extended her hand. I took it. It was a cold dead thing. I wanted it to tremble. I wanted it to be a sparrow again. I wanted to believe that I hadn't helped in draining the life from her.

"Thank you for trying, Diana, but it's too late." She hurried away.

A palm frond tickled my cheek as I watched The Tantrum watch Julie tilt her head back, open her mouth, and swallow an oyster. She'd finally found something to eat. He let out one of his happy-baby giggles then dipped his forefinger into the bowl of caviar and began to greedily suck it.

I made my way across the room to James. The cinematographer's eyes were now at half-mast. He was using the wall to prop himself up.

James peered over his dark glasses at his party as if he were studying a scene he couldn't get right.

"Diana, you finally came over to greet your host," he said as if I had been the flaw.

"It's a lovely party."

"But?" He talked in the quiet bland tone of a man who was used to dealing with other people's emotions.

"Carol asked me to tell you that she's gone up to the room. Could we talk alone?" I glanced at Marcus who was now resting his chin on his chest.

James grinned at him. "We are alone. What do you want to talk about? The earrings I gave Julie?"

"You heard?"

"Actors whisper so loudly."

"But you and I know you didn't give them to her."

Marcus muttered what sounded like the word 'glare' then slid down the wall and sat on the floor. Since Marcus usually ended up on the floor no one paid him any attention.

James peered at me over his sunglasses. "When did I stop being a genius, Diana?"

"I'm worried about your wife, not your career," I spoke more bluntly than I had intended.

"So am I. Carol was willing to believe a genius. But she isn't willing to believe a hack. That's why I'm standing here trying to figure out when I stopped being a genius. Was it two movies ago?"

"I'm afraid Carol is going to do something drastic."

He tilted his head as if to get a better angle on his career. "How could I not recognize the fact that I'm not a genius anymore? Carol did. Was it three movies ago?"

"You still have it," I lied. "They're talking Oscar for Julie." I had to stop saying that. I had to leave this alone. I had to take my shoes off.

"I have a new project in the works," he said, momentarily forgetting he wasn't a genius anymore. "It's about two men and a Buffalo."

"Really?"

"There's the part of a zoologist you're perfect for. I'll get a script to you when we get back to L.A."

"Thanks." So I'd work again. The actor's salvation.

"Strike the glare," Marcus announced, blinking up at us.

"Julie thinks I'm a genius," James observed, adjusting his dark glasses.

"Of course she does."

I was suddenly exhausted. I excused myself and went up to my room.

Around two thirty in the morning I awoke to someone knocking on my door and the sound of Carol Barron's voice in the hallway. I threw on a robe, turned on the desk lamp, and opened the door. Carol walked in and sat on the sofa. She wore a quilted blue silk bathrobe and stared at the gun in her hand as if she'd picked up the wrong evening bag.

"He lost his touch," she said.

Julie appeared in the doorway still dressed in her lime-green gown. "You bitch!" she screamed at Carol. The earrings shimmered. A few hotel guests, disturbed by the noise, peered sleepily out into the hall. I jerked Julie into the room and shut the door.

"What happened?" I demanded.

"Most wives leave. They take the money and leave," Julie said, furiously pacing back and forth.

"Even your pacing is a cliché," Carol observed dryly.

"Where's James?" I asked.

"He lost his touch," Carol repeated, rubbing her forehead.

"He's dead. Where do you think he is?!" Julie stamped her foot.

"He's in her bedroom," Carol spoke calmly. "Sprawled on the floor by the bathroom door. He was trying to hide from me in there. Another cliché."

I held out my hand to her. "Give me the gun."

"I can't do that, Diana."

"Give her the gun," Julie demanded.

Carol pointed the barrel of the gun at Julie. "I can't do that until I figure out which one of us is the bigger cliché. The Girlfriend or The Wife?"

Julie froze, eyes narrowing with fear. "What is she talking about, Diana?"

"She's wondering which one of you is less meaningful, or more hackneyed." My voice sounded unreal, empty of all emotion, like a United Nations interpreter.

"What does that have to do with anything? And how about, Diana? She had an affaire with him too," she whined, pointing at me.

"James didn't give her earrings from Tiffany's."

"But I found them in a snow bank."

"Be quiet!" Carol snapped.

Tears began to roll down Julie's cheeks. "It's true. Tell her, Diana."

Carol tilted her drawn pale face up to mine. "Don't, Diana. Don't tell me. Just get the earrings from her." She waved the gun at me.

I brushed back Julie's hair from her wet face. While she cried I unscrewed the post from behind her left ear and slipped the diamond and emerald earring from her lobe. Then I did the same with the right one. I handed them to Carol.

"You don't want to harm anyone else," I pleaded with her. "Please, give me the gun."

"I have to put an end to it, Diana." She weighed the earrings in her hand. "These insult my intelligence."

"I just thought James could help me with my career. Like Woody Allen and Diane Keaton," Julie was talking frantically now. "I wanted to be a movie star ... Everybody wants that ... And everybody has affaires ... So why do you want to kill me? They're talking Oscar ... And I did find them in a snow bank ... I did ... I did ..."

"Oh, shut up," Carol said in a weary voice. The gun exploded.

I jerked back. Julie's hands flew up to her face. Carol dropped the gun and grabbed at the bright red wound between her breasts. She pitched forward onto the floor. I knelt down and held her hand; it quivered in mine and then it didn't. I gathered up the earrings.

Peering over her fingertips Julie began to babble, "She didn't kill me ... she killed herself ... not me ... not me ..."

I went over and slapped her hard. Stunned, she fell silent.

I left her. Ignoring the disconcerted expressions of the guests once again peeking from their rooms, I walked down the hall to Julie's suite. The door was ajar. I walked through the sitting room into the bedroom, stepped around the body of the man who had lost his touch, and took the little blue box off her dresser. Placing the earrings inside of it, I dropped the box into the pocket of my robe. I called the Tantrum. He took charge of getting Julie and me new rooms. He gave her sleeping pills so she wouldn't have to talk to the police. It was left for me to deal with them.

In the early dawn I sat alone in my room and stared at the little blue box. I was waiting.

I was waiting for Tiffany's to open.

Aimlessly channel surfing, I was standing in my kitchen wearing sweats, hair pulled back, and no makeup, gathering my courage to go into my office to write. Then I saw myself on the screen acting in the series Bewitched. *After I got over the shock of how young, beautiful and filled with hope I had been, I realized that all the lead actors in the series were dead. The dead were rerunning. In fact, TV is filled with the talking dead. I went into my office and began to write this short story.*

THE TALKING DEAD

"And last but not least I would like to thank my father who loved his booze more than me. But when he was half-sober and feeling melancholy he would take me out in the backyard at night and teach me to talk to the moon. Thanks, Dad." Tears filling his eyes, Brendan Kincaid raised his Golden Globe in the air and bowed to the audience, the TV cameras, and the world. I adjusted my pearls and black silk suit jacket and forced an appropriate smile. Even for an actor, Brendan Kincaid cried too easily.

As the ballroom filled with applause I peered around the glittering centerpiece on the table and nodded at Alison, Brendan's wife. Kneeling in front of her like a suitor about to propose marriage was a man in a tuxedo, balancing a camera on his shoulder, capturing her tired but triumphant expression.

"Oh, Diana, Brendan is so sensitive," the young – some say too young – actress, who played Brendan's TV wife, gushed into my ear.

I am one of those who say she is too young. But that's because I tried out for the role of Brendan's wife and didn't get it. I wasn't age appropriate meaning I was too old, meaning I was Brendan's age.

"I love how he talks about his life. Don't you?" She beamed. I nodded politely even though I didn't agree. Brendan talked about his life as if no one else had one.

The fickle cameraman moved away from Kincaid's wife and focused on the young actress. She began to applaud wildly. I know all the tricks of the acting trade, but again I marveled at how quickly tears appeared in her creaseless eyes. If there is one more award show, I thought, Hollywood would drown in its own tears of adulation. Maybe I *was* too old.

Sitting on my right was Theodora Woods; she had just accepted her own Golden Globe for being the creator of the newest, hottest sitcom: *The Life of Brendan Kincaid.* She also happened to be Brendan's lover. I was her guest at the table. Theo liked my work and always made sure there was a part for me in her shows. I nodded and smiled at Theo. The cameraman now pointed his lens at her. But she wasn't applauding and she wasn't smiling. As the star-filled audience, clad in tuxedos and evening gowns, got to their feet giving Brendan a standing ovation, Theodora remained seated; her intelligent dark eyes shined with betrayal. Her short dark hair was cut at sharp angles. Her mouth, lipstick long forgotten, was pressed into a thin resentful line. The cameraman, not one for nuance, lurched away toward another more easily identifiable face.

"What's wrong?" I whispered in her ear.

"TV saps your soul." She downed the last of her wine and placed her napkin firmly on the table. The thin strap of her purple velvet gown slipped from her bony shoulder as she stood and stalked with great purpose out of the Grand Ballroom. A frown deepened the lines around Alison Kincaid's eyes as she watched Theo leave. In shock, the young actress' tears dried immediately as if they were made out of polyester.

Theodora Woods forgot to take her award.

People don't walk out in Hollywood. They are pushed out, kicking and screaming and clutching their multi-million dollar golden parachutes. So when Theo got up and left during a standing ovation for the star of her show it was an unsettling event. Even Brendan was rendered speechless upon his return to the table. It was quickly decided that Theo must not have been feeling well and I, her friend, should take her award home for safe-keeping. They considered me her friend because Theo got me work.

Since my husband Colin died of a heart attack I live alone in our unremodeled beach house – euphemistically called a teardown – in Malibu. That night I placed Theo's award on the mantle next to Colin's two Oscars, which he had won for best screenplay. The two awards and the house were all I had left. Having to earn a living, I had gone back to what I knew best: acting.

I called Theo and got her machine. After leaving a message I crawled into bed, took my sleeping pill, and turned on the TV. There was nothing I wanted to watch; I just wanted to fill the silence even while I slept. Closing my eyes I wondered what Theo was doing. She wasn't the kind of woman you worried about; but her behavior, even for a writer, was odd.

The next morning I was standing in my kitchen drinking coffee and channel surfing my way to the news when on some obscure station I saw the shocking image of myself at eighteen. I was acting in a segment of *Bewitched*. Samantha, the witch, was wiggling her nose, trying to turn me into an ugly old hag so Darrin, her husband, would not be attracted to me. I no longer knew that young blonde-haired woman who was once me. Her face was filled with such hope and beauty that she broke my heart. She also looked young enough to be Brendan Kincaid's TV wife. The doorbell rang. Pulling my husband's paisley silk robe more tightly around me, I ran my hand through my now determinedly blonde hair and went to answer it.

Brendan Kincaid burst in. "Where is Theo?"

"I don't know."

Brendan was tall and woodenly handsome. He reached out his arms in a hopelessly dramatic gesture that reeked of bad acting; it was his larger than life mannerisms which had no connection to the reality of the moment that made Brendan such a comic success on the small screen.

"I've been calling her all night. I keep getting the machine. I went to her house this morning and she's not there." He peered forlornly down at the little alligator-insignia on his pink polo shirt as if it might help him.

"Maybe she's already at the studio," I offered.

"I tried her office. Nothing. Nobody has seen her. I thought she might've come here to pick up her award."

"No." He followed my gaze to the fireplace mantel.

"You put her award with Colin's Oscars?"

"I thought her sense of irony might like that."

"Are you saying my show is beneath the writing of the great Colin?"

"Yes." You could be honest with Brendan because he never listened to what you said.

"I've been up all night," he groaned. "I need a cup of coffee."

He followed me into the kitchen and slumped in a chair. "What happened, Diana? Why did she get up and leave like that? The Golden Globes for God's sake, and just as I'm getting a standing ovation. I mean it was her standing ovation, too. I was gracious in my acceptance speech, wasn't I?" His big brown spaniel eyes pleaded with me.

"Mentioning your father was very touching. As usual you were very charming, Brendan."

"What do you mean as usual? You've never liked me, have you?"

"I don't know what Theo sees in you."

"Since Colin died you've turned into a very bitter woman, Diana Poole. It's not my fault he left you with no money."

"Money never mattered to us. You're married, Brendan."

"So? If that's your reason for disliking a man you must ..." Again he waved his arm dramatically in the air searching for the words to finish his sentence. Letting his arm fall to his side he gave up the search. I handed him a cup of coffee and sat down across from him. He took a sip and stared at the TV.

"You watch *Bewitched*?"

"No. I was channel surfing and saw my ..."

"Who is that?"

"Who?"

He leaned forward squinting at the young me on the screen. "The blonde. The voice is familiar."

"Are you being funny?"

"God, she's gorgeous. Can you imagine what she looks like now?"

"No, I can't."

He dragged his hand through his thick brown hair leaving it askew. This gesture always brought gales of laughter from the TV audience.

"Do you realize that every one of those stars on *Bewitched* are dead now?" he said bleakly. "I mean if you think about it they're just dead people talking."

"Sounds like something Theo would say." I grabbed the remote and turned the TV off. The young me vanished.

"I said it. Not Theo," he snapped.

"All right. You said it."

"What do you mean, 'I'm married'? Is that why Theo walked out? She wants me to divorce Alison? Did she tell you that?"

"No."

"Then what did you mean by that crack?"

"It wasn't a crack. It's a fact. You are a married man. And it's taking a toll on Theo. Not to mention your wife."

"Oh God, this should be the happiest morning of my life but I have you moralizing at me, and I can't find Theo. What possessed her, Diana?"

"When you were in her house did you look in the closet and see if she packed some of her clothes?"

"How would I know? Theo isn't the kind of woman that makes you pay attention to what she wears. In fact she has awful taste in clothes. Did you see that purple thing she was wearing last night?"

"Did she take a suitcase?"

He shrugged helplessly.

"I'll go look. I have a key."

"You have a key?"

"She's five houses down from me on the beach. I look after her place while she's gone and she looks after mine."

"Yes, but I didn't know you had a key," he said, in a proprietary voice.

"When she's traveling I pick up the newspapers and water the plants. She does the same for me when I'm on location. What's wrong with that?"

"Nothing, I just didn't know that's all. I think of it as our little hideaway. Hers and mine."

"It's her home, Brendan. She bought and paid for it."

"Why do you resent me?" He rested his chin in his hand.

"In all honesty? I don't know. You're charming. You have a wonderful way of expressing yourself, and an inept way of acting that people respond to. Theo says she loves you. Your wife stays with you. Your fans adore you. By all rights I should like you too, but I don't."

He eyed me suspiciously. "Did you talk her into leaving me?"

"Nobody talks Theo into anything."

"That's true. She must've said something, Diana, when she got up and left last night."

"She said: 'TV saps your soul.'"

"TV saps your soul?"

"Yes."

"TV?"

"TV."

"What does it mean?"

"I think it means that Theo is tired, burnt-out. The last time we had lunch she mentioned she wanted to get away and write her novel."

"A novel?"

"A book."

"I know what a novel is. You don't have to be so condescending."

"I'm sorry. You bring it out in me. She probably went away to think."

"Either way I lose."

"There are other writers, Brendan."

"Not like her."

"There are even other lovers."

"Do you really believe I don't care for her? That I could just transfer my needs and affection to somebody else? I don't think you know what Theo means to me. She gave me the strength to talk about my father last night. She brings things out in me I never thought were significant. She sees the significance in me."

All actors feel inferior. So when an actor finds someone, especially a writer, who sees the worth in him that is much more important than mere love. I know. I was an actor married to a writer.

"Did you two have an argument?" I asked.

"No. Yes, but not about us, about words."

"The show?"

"It was about the way I say my lines, or her lines. She's very possessive about her lines."

"Writer's are protective of their words."

"It's just dialogue, Diana. Nothing more. You don't think she's had a breakdown, do you?" He buried his face in hands. "Oh, God, I can't go on without her."

"Actors always go on."

He peered over his fingertips at me. "Did you just make that up? I mean just now, off the top of your head?"

"Yes."

"That was very funny," he said, not laughing. "But do you think it's true?"

"That actors always go on? Yes."

"I hope you're right. 'TV saps your soul.' How could Theo say that? It's given me mine."

"TV has given you steady work, money and fame, Brendan. But not your soul. I'm not so sure you have one."

He smiled his charming lop-sided grin. "Sometimes I think you know me best, Diana."

I smiled back. You couldn't help it with Brendan. He took another sip of his coffee then spoke with a dark finality, "That was an omen."

"What was?"

"You watching the rerun of *Bewitched*. Dead people talking." He got slowly to his feet and wandered out of my house.

Later I walked down the beach to Theo's and let myself in with her key. In the living room her sparse expensive stiff-backed furniture looked stoic and prim like lonely women who have waited too long to say 'yes'. The house was heavy with silence. But her house was always quiet. I, who must have the TV or music on all the time, once asked her how she could stand the silence. Theo pointed to her head and said, "It's not quiet in here. I'm a writer. I love it." I had laughed, remembering my husband sitting in the stillness of his office; a room I hardly go into anymore. And now there was no Theo, with her eyes turned inward, moving gracefully through her silence toward her office.

I quickly went into her bedroom and searched through her closet. Her suitcase was gone and so were some of her clothes. I heard the front door open and close; then hurried footsteps in the hall. I waited listening. Drawers were being opened and slammed shut in her office. I crept down the hallway and peered in.

Brendan Kincaid was taking papers from her filing cabinet and placing them into a large plastic trash bag.

"Hello, Brendan." I leaned against the door jam.

"God, Diana, you scared the hell out of me. I didn't see your car."

"I walked down the beach. I told you I was going to check to see if she took a suitcase with her."

"Did she?" He dumped some folders into the bag.

"Yes. What are you doing?"

"I don't think she's coming back."

"You didn't answer my question. What are you doing taking her papers?"

"I've written her love letters. I don't think that's anybody's business but mine. I want to find Theo. Not cause my wife embarrassment."

"You wrote a trash bag full of love letters?"

"And the scripts are mine, just as much as they are hers." He stuffed more papers into the bag. A card fluttered to the ground.

"You're acting like she's not coming back, Brendan."

"I don't think she can forgive me."

"For what?"

"Stealing ... her love." Throwing the trash bag over his shoulder he lurched down the hallway and out the front door.

"You have no right to take any of this, Brendan," I foolishly yelled after him, but he wasn't listening.

In Hollywood everybody has a right. It's all about rights: the rights of the stars, the rights of the director, the rights of the producer. Even the rights of the lover. It's all about how many rights you can accumulate in your contract or how many you can steal.

I picked up the card he had dropped. It was a warm and fuzzy drugstore card declaring eternal love and was signed by Brendan. Where love letters were concerned he was certainly no Browning. I checked the back of the card to see if he had sent her a Hallmark and discovered the words: 'Dead people talking'. They were written in Theo's hand. And they were the exact words Brendan had used this morning when watching *Bewitched*. I placed the card on her desk.

It was a Hallmark.

That night something jarred me out of my sleep. My heart pounding, I sat up feeling another's presence in my room. I quickly turned on the light. It was only W.C Fields in the movie *David Copperfield* falling downstairs and announcing that he had arrived. As usual I had fallen asleep with the TV on. I felt comforted by Fields until I remembered he was one of the dead people talking. I got out of bed, threw on a robe, went into the living room, and opened the sliding glass door. On the deck I breathed in the heavy salty air and watched the dark waves turn white as they splattered on the shore in the moonlight. I gazed down the beach toward Theo's house. A light shone in the window. Had she come back?

I slipped into some shoes, threw on a coat, got her key, ran down the beach and let myself in. In the dark I made my way through to her office. Alison Kincaid was going through Theo's computer discs.

"Hello, Diana," she greeted. Her face was strained and pale. "Thought you'd be asleep. Brendan is not computer literate. Didn't think to get her discs." She looked through them with a clerical precision.

"What's all this about, Alison?"

"Theo's not coming back. At least not to Brendan."

"How do you know?"

"He received a post card from her. It was placed in the mailbox, not sent. It has a picture of the Grauman's Chinese Theatre on it. Do they still call it Graumans?"

"I think it's a Lowes now. Who knows what they call things anymore." "Here, read it." She whipped it out of her pocket and thrust it at me. It read: 'Brendan, you tried standing in mine now you're going to have to find another pair. Here's a graveyard full of them.' I turned it over. It was a post card of all the old movie star's footprints.

"He's frantic, Diana." Alison opened her tote bag and dumped the computer discs into it.

"What possible use can her personal writings be to you?" I grabbed a yellow legal tablet out of her hand. "You just can't take anything you want."

"I have to fill a void!" she snapped, pointing a bony-manicured finger at me. Her gray eyes were desperate. "Fifteen years ago I married the most beautiful actor in the world. A handsome void. I thought I could fill him with love. I couldn't. When Theo came to him with this idea for a show he slowly began to change. Then he started to have an affair with her. That's when he became a different man. The man that I had always wanted. Witty and sharp. Why do you think I put up with the affair? I don't want to lose that witty and wise man, Diana. I have to help him."

"Help him do what?"

"Fill the void." She snapped her bag shut and walked briskly out of Theo's house.

I sighed and leafed through the yellow legal size tablet; it was a writer's sketchbook. There was a brief description of a woman having coffee. Ideas for different books. Observations. Overheard conversations that Theo had jotted down. From her desk I took the greeting card Brendan had given her and turned it over. 'Dead people talking.' Why had she written that phrase on Brendan's card? Did she think he was one of the dead people? Or did she just use the card to make her writer's note? I replaced it and took the yellow legal pad home with me. I fell asleep looking through it while *David Copperfield* found that his first true love was not all that she was cracked up to be.

The next morning I was standing in my kitchen watching the local news when the image of Brendan Kincaid appeared in a room filled with microphones and reporters. He announced that the he was asking the police for their help in finding Theodora Woods. He looked exhausted and scared. Why was he so frightened? At the end of the news conference he peered into the camera and said, "I know this may sound odd coming from me, but I think it's important to say. TV CAN SAP YOUR SOUL. It's such hard work, you don't get to see your loved ones, and there is always the pressure of the next show. I think, I hope, that Theo is somewhere getting in touch with her soul again and that she will soon return to us and those who love her. Come back to us, Theo. With your soul intact."

A few hours later Brendan called me. "Have you heard anything?"

"No."

"She's not coming back. I have to adjust. Prepare."

"For what?"

"My wife said she ran into you last night."

"You mean while she was ransacking Theo's office?"

"We don't want you to mention that to the police when they talk to you. Remember, Diana, you need to work in this town."

"Is that a threat?"

"I don't know. It seemed the appropriate thing to say."

"*Appropriate*? Brendan can you hear yourself?"

"Oh, God, I'm so lost without her."

"Are you aware that you used Theo's words as your own in the press conference?"

"What do you mean?"

"'TV saps your soul.'"

"How can you be so petty at a time like this?" He hung up on me.

I poured myself another cup of coffee, put on a CD of Willie Nelson croaking about love, sat down in the living room, and went page by page through Theo's note pad. I was looking for a clue, a hint of why she had walked out. Under the title *A Life* I read: My father was a drunk. He loved the sauce more than he loved me. But when he was half sober and feeling melancholy he would take me out in the backyard and we would sit on the damp grass while he taught me how to talk to the moon.

Had she written down a vignette from Brendan's life or from her own? I stared at the Golden Globe sitting on the mantle. It looked like it had been moved. Did Brendan pick it up when he was here? I couldn't remember. At one o'clock I had an interview for an antacid commercial. So I went and changed into what I call my good-wife clothes: slacks, pastel colored print blouse, and Keds. In the script my dopey husband didn't know when to stop eating.

It was six o'clock when I returned to the house. After the interview I had run errands and gone to the market. I didn't get the commercial. I guess I wasn't that good of a wife.

Late that night sipping a glass of wine I walked out onto the deck and again looked toward Theo's house; it was dark. I wondered just what Theo was doing by putting that post card in Brendan's mailbox? Was she playing some kind of cruel psychological game with him? If so, she didn't have to leave town for that. Now that Brendan and his wife had ransacked her files the last place anyone would look for her very late at night would be her own home. I got her key and my flashlight.

"Theo?" I called, entering her house. My light bounced around her living room. "Theo?" I moved down the hallway to her bedroom. "Theo?" I turned the overhead light on. Brendan Kincaid lay on her bed surrounded by more of Theo's papers. His arms flayed out in one of his helpless gestures. Blood ran from a dark hole in his temple down his neck and into his shirt collar. On the floor by the bed was a gun. I leaned against the wall for support. The poor guy looked like he had been sitting on the bed studying her writings as if they were cliff notes, as if he had a test he knew he wasn't going to pass. I stumbled back down the hall and to the phone in the kitchen.

Three hours later wearing my husband's bathrobe I sat alone in my living room. I had told the police everything I knew. Alison was called. She had recognized the gun as belonging to Brendan. The two detectives were talking suicide. I offered to go home with Alison but she refused.

"You were Theo's friend not Brendan's," she had told me. "Theo caused his suicide. She wanted it to happen."

But why? And where was Theo? Staring at her award on the mantelpiece I realized I had been sitting in complete silence. I had forgotten to turn on the TV or my CD player. Folding my arms across my chest I stood in front of the fireplace. The Two Oscars were sleek in their art deco streamline gold-plated nudity. The Golden Globe looked bold in its artlessness. A chill ran through me. The award *had* been moved. Even Theo couldn't resist touching it.

I walked slowly, like a pall barer, through my kitchen to the room that was once my husband's office. Trembling I opened the door and quickly flipped on the light. His desk chair was at a quarter-turn as if he had just stood up. My photograph was still on his desk. The computer screen was blank. The daybed appeared to be untouched. The small bathroom still had the faint smell of Colin's cologne. I breathed it in feeling the pain of loss once more. I opened the door that led out to the side of the house. The walkway was as it should be. Everything was as it should be. And yet something was wrong. Colin's room did not have the feel of a forgotten place. There was the sense of someone having recently been in it. Of the stillness having been broken.

I took Theo's award from the mantel and went back to my room. I placed it on my nightstand and got into bed. I turned off the light. I didn't turn on the television. I didn't take my sleeping pill. I stared at the shadows on the ceiling and waited in the dark terrifying quiet. I'm not sure how much time had passed when I saw Theo's slim figure in my doorway.

"It took me a while to figure out what was wrong," she said in her low soft voice. "No TV, no Willie Nelson. No white noise."

"You were counting on my fear of silence." I sat up and turned on the light. We blinked as if seeing each other for the first time. She wore black slacks and a black sweater. Her small sharp face was drawn. Her intelligent eyes looked dull. I'd never seen her eyes look dull before.

"I was only taking advantage of your fear. Why are you so afraid, Diana?" She stayed in the doorway.

"Just like Brendan I'm trying to a fill a void. The void death makes."

"I liked staying in Colin's room. It was like sleeping in a shrine."

"You've been here all the time."

"Yes. I hope you don't mind. I just needed to be where nobody could get at me. Haven't you ever felt like that, Diana?" She titled her head and attempted a smile.

"I think you needed to be in a place where you could commit a murder and nobody would know."

"What are you talking about?"

"Brendan's dead."

"Brendan? I don't believe it." She sagged against the door jam; writers should never act.

"Writers should never act," I said.

She pulled herself up to her full height.

"That's better."

"How did he die?" she asked.

"The police think he committed suicide in your house. But I don't believe he killed himself. Of course they're waiting to talk to you." I swung my legs around and sat on the edge of the bed.

"How can you think I would do such a thing? My God, did Brendan think I was never coming back?" she asked.

"Maybe it was the postcard you sent him."

"I was angry at him, but not enough to kill him, Diana."

"You knew I rarely went into Colin's office. You knew I hated a silent house. What did you do with your car? Park it on a side street?"

"Unless you have proof I wouldn't go around saying things like that. You know how this town talks. Besides what's my motive? Brendan was making me a fortune, and he was my lover."

"Brendan would have left you with nothing to write about."

She laughed harshly. "That's hardly a motive, Diana."

"But it's true. Dorothy Parker said, 'give me a man that is handsome, ruthless and stupid.' Well, that was your Brendan. And you liked that about him. But the more successful he became the more he felt he needed to talk off-screen like he did on-screen. He began to repeat things you had shared with him about your life as if they were his own, didn't he?"

Rubbing her forehead she paused a moment then said evenly, "I thought I had found what every writer, hell, every woman, hopes for. A lover that is a good listener. But I got suckered. I would hear him at parties talking about his father but it was really my father. His father drank diet cola and ate macaroni and cheese and never said an interesting thing in his life. My father was a drunk but at least he talked to the moon. Brendan would make a witty observation, everyone would laugh, but it was my observation. How do you tell a person at a dinner party that's not really Brendan speaking, that's me? You can't without sounding like a petty idiot."

"He needed to fill his own void. That's what his wife said."

"She knew him better than I did. I began to realize he was stealing my life, my creative life, so he could fill his empty one. You're correct about one thing, Diana. I was afraid I'd have nothing left to write when I sat down to start my novel. I couldn't shut him up. I couldn't stop him. I tried but he just didn't see the problem. It was all dialogue to him."

"But you did stop him."

"Nobody will believe that I killed Brendan. The golden goose never gets killed in Hollywood."

"You killed this one. You got him to come to your house. That would be easy. But how did you get his gun? That's the only part I can't figure out."

"Are you telling me he shot himself with his own gun? He must've used the gun he gave me. Brendan didn't like the thought of me alone at the beach without protection. Diana, I've been good to you. I given you parts in my shows that other actresses your age would kill for."

"Well, this show is over, isn't it? You've seen to that."

"I'll write other shows, other parts."

"But Theo, even with Brendan dead you still won't be able to write your novel."

Her dull eyes glimmered briefly with the pain of recognition. "Why do you say that?"

"If TV saps your soul what does murder do to it?"

"TV is worse. Trust me." She grinned wryly. It was Theo at her ironical best.

"I want my key back."

"Sure." She reached in her pocket of her slacks took the key and dropped it on my dresser.

"Yours is there in the glass bowl."

She took it.

"Don't forget your Golden Globe."

Theo picked it up and weighed it in her hand staring at me all the time.

"Are you thinking of killing me, too?"

"No, you have no proof. Except that Brendan was sucking all my creativity out of me. And who is going to buy that as a motive in Hollywood? People get paid for doing that here. It's called synergy."

"Alison Kincaid may think as I do."

"No. She loved the man Brendan had become. The Brendan I had created. She wouldn't want his image tarnished."

"Where are you going to go?" I asked.

"To the police. Tell them how shocked I am. And hope that my silly behavior wasn't partly to blame for his suicide. But sometimes, Diana, a woman just needs to get away. She just needs to pull her thoughts together. Goodnight."

I made sure Theo had left and then I went back to bed. I turned on the TV. Bette Davis was talking. On reruns of his show Brendan Kincaid would soon be talking again. Now Theo too was one of the talking dead; she just didn't know it yet. Cold, I pulled the covers up around me and watched Bette Davis blow smoke.

Trying on clothes in a department store dressing room I heard a mother and a daughter arguing over a dress the mother wanted the daughter to buy. I was stunned by the lack of compassion in the mother's voice and the hurtful anger of the daughter as they battled each other. I didn't buy anything, but I came away with an idea for a short story. How far would a daughter go to please her mother? How far would a mother go to get her way with her daughter?

THE GOOD DAUGHTER

"Diana, tell Kyra how beautiful she looks," Monique Lancer told me.

Kyra, Monique's daughter, fought back tears as she glared at her reflection in the bedroom mirror. I sat in a silk slipper chair sipping wine.

"It won't do any good, Diana," Kyra snapped. "I'm not wearing this stupid dress." A small figure of a winged angel was tattooed on the curve of her young breast.

"Tell her, Diana."

Monique squeezed my hand; it was a cold bony reminder that she was one of the most powerful agents in Hollywood. And she had just gotten me a role in a movie with the hot new young actor Jimmy Whitelaw. I had ten lines and had just finished shooting my part. I knew I was on treacherous ground. Not only was I being inserted into the middle of an argument between a mother and daughter, but I was also being commanded to lie. I needed work so I considered what it would morally cost me to tell a sixteen-year-old girl that she didn't look ridiculous in an evening gown when she did. The gown was a pink strapless affair with a huge ruffled skirt that swept the floor. Scarlet O'Hara going to a 1950's prom came to mind. Except for the tattoo on her breast. While I was trying to find the right complimentary words without sounding like a sycophant, Kyra turned her hard little face on her mother.

"Who is this birthday party for? You or me?"

"You, darling, I've already been sixteen. I see no problem with having some of my friends here."

"You don't have friends. You have famous clients."

"Diana is my friend."

"She's hoping you'll take her on as a client. Why don't you tell her what you told me? S he's too old!" Now Kyra glared at me.

"I said it would be difficult to take Diana on because there are so few roles for women on the verge of middle-age."

On the verge? They went on this way, talking about me as if I weren't there. Just to make sure I checked my reflection in the mirror. Yes, I was in Kyra's bedroom sitting in the blue silk slipper chair, my long legs crossed, wearing a black suit that showed off my fleshy curves, and determinedly blonde hair. I could hear guests arriving in the foyer below.

Monique, thin as a sliver of ice, thrust a pink barrette into her daughter's harshly dyed black hair. The severe color turned Kyra's flawless pale skin a dead white.

I took more wine. I was drinking too much. I was drinking in place of good acting roles, in place of sex, in place of a man in my bed, in place of letting go of my dead husband. I was avoiding the void.

Kyra screamed the name, "Jimmy Whitelaw!" drawing my attention back to mother and daughter.

"That's who this party is for. Jimmy Whitelaw. Not me! You're just using me."

Jimmy had the enormous ego of a very little man. When I had worked with him he had to stand on what the crew calls an apple box to make him taller. We all had to pretend he didn't have to stand on it. Jimmy loved call- girls. He bragged about having them dress in retro fifties style cheerleader outfits or prom gowns. I looked at Kyra wearing her pink pouf of a ball gown. My heart sank.

"Is this dress you're forcing her to wear about Jimmy Whitelaw?" I asked Monique.

"He's taken a liking to Kyra. Who wouldn't?" she fluffed her daughter's hair. Kyra recoiled from her mother's touch.

"He doesn't like women," I said.

"I knew he was a creep," Kyra said.

"Be quiet," her mother said, and then stared me down. "He likes women, Diana."

"He's short," Kyra snapped.

"I know the production company paid to have him surrounded by three prostitutes on the set. It's amazing what keeps the costs of making movies so high and my salary so low."

"You got that part thanks to me. And so what if he likes call-girls?"

"He likes them dressed the way you've dressed Kyra."

"You want me to go to bed with him! You think that will get him as a client," Kyra fumed. But no tears of a mother's betrayal showed in her eyes. They could have been fighting over, well, a dress.

"It's not as if you're a virgin. You might as well get something for it instead of giving it away free."

"You can't tell me what to do with my body."

"Oh, for God's sake you call sex "hooking-up." Having sex means nothing to you. And I might add who pays the bills? Who keeps your way of life going?"

As mother and daughter began to go at one another again I picked up my wine glass and purse. At the bedroom door I said:

"Kyra, that's the ugliest gown I have ever seen. Don't wear it. If you do you'll regret it your entire life."

I walked out of the bedroom. Pausing on the long curve of stairs I peered down at the famous guests mingling in the marble foyer. There was an over abundance of facelifts. The pulled skin on the women and men shined synthetically in the light of the crystal chandelier. The stars that were invited to Kyra's Sweet Sixteen Birthday party were dimming. Monique Lancer's clients were getting old. She needed young blood. She needed Jimmy Whitelaw.

"Diana," Monique grabbed my arm. "Don't you ever tell my daughter what to do. And she's not some innocent child either."

"And she's not some deal you're hawking either."

I pulled away from her. Jimmy Whitelaw rushed up the stairs. Not recognizing me, his gaze quickly shifted to the top of the landing and Kyra's door.

"Is that her room?" he asked Monique. Anticipation made his voice higher.

She nodded. He continued up the steps and slipped into the bedroom. The deal was done.

"I'm going home."

Standing under the portico I asked the valet for my car. He stared at me as if I were crazy.

"Sorry, ma'am. We have all these limos coming in. It'll be awhile."

"I'll wait."

I stood there greeting people that I knew and being avoided by others that I also knew. You're never sure why you're being shunned in Hollywood; that's what makes it so insidious. I gave up waiting and walked around the side of the house.

Under the enormous marquee a rap band was performing. The noise was deafening and had all the rhythm of an Uzi. Bodyguards with guns tucked under their heavy leather jackets surrounded the stage, protecting the rappers from the famous white audience. I walked across the lawn to the infinity pool; it looked like it was spilling Monique's purified sewage over the hills of Hollywood. The rapper's sounds filled the rich night air leaving no room for any other sound. There were guards placed around the property. Most of the men securing the party were moonlighting LAPD officers. There was only one who looked comfortable in his suit. He stood by the pool, hands in his pant pockets, looking out at the city lights.

"You a detective?" I asked, trying to talk over the music.

"What?" His dark eyes assessed me like a piece of evidence. He stepped closer in order to hear me.

I repeated my question.

"Yes. How did you know?"

"You look like you're used to wearing a suit."

He laughed. His dark hair was cut short and graying at the temples. He had a high forehead and a nose that looked like it had taken a punch. Men, I thought ruefully. Give them a bashed nose and it only makes them look more intriguing. The music thumped and pestered.

"I didn't know detectives moonlighted. I thought it was mostly motorcycle cops."

"I need the money. Ex-wife. Actually three ex wives."

"I can't hear. Did you say three?"

He nodded sheepishly. Then cupped his mouth with his hand and spoke into my ear. "Should I know who you are?" His warm breath tickled my neck. His crooked smile came easily.

"No."

"But I have seen you in the movies."

"Probably. You just didn't know it was me."

"And who is me?"

"What?"

"Your name?" he yelled.

"Diana Poole."

He repeated my name trying to place me. "I have seen you. But you're right I didn't know it was you. Do you want to know who I am?"

"Not if you're somebody."

"Just a detective."

"You could be a singing detective."

"Who?"

"A singing ... Never mind," I shouted. "What's your name?"

"My name? Leo Heath."

"You lied."

"What?"

"You lied! You wrote a book that was made into a movie."

"Did you read it?" He looked surprised.

"No."

"See the movie?"

"No. I read for a part in the movie. I didn't get it. You earned a ton of money. What are you doing moonlighting?"

"As I said, I have three ex-wives."

"Write another book."

"What?"

"Write another book!" I screamed. The music stopped.

My words hung in the air. My ears rang. We laughed.

"I can't," he said in his normal voice, which was surprisingly soft and intimate. I wondered if the tone of his voice made it easier for him to extract the truth from criminals and victims.

"Why can't you?"

"I have writer's block. Hey, where are you going?"

"You're too famous for me. Besides my ears are ringing and I want to go home," I said, trying to ignore my body's response to his.

"And where is that?"

"Malibu."

"You must have three very wealthy ex-husbands." He grinned.

"Very perceptive." I returned his smile.

I looked up at the glowing lamp in Kyra's bedroom window and decided I couldn't leave just yet. Somebody had to look after her.

The foyer was empty. All the guests were in the back yard. I went up the stairs and knocked on her door. There was no answer. I went in. The room was empty. Just the pink prom-like gown on the floor; the bodice collapsed into its full skirt. The skirt billowed out on the carpet as if it had just parachuted to earth.

Monique swept in. "Where is Kyra?" she demanded.

"I don't know."

"What are you doing in here?"

"I came to see if she was all right. Is that why you're here?"

"Have you seen Jimmy Whitelaw?"

"No."

Her narrow face tightened into anger. "She didn't wear the dress. One of the guests said they saw Kyra outside standing by herself. She was wearing jeans and a sweater. Damn her."

"For a moment I thought you might be worried about her."

"I'm disappointed in you, Diana. I thought you were more sophisticated than you really are."

"You call prostituting your daughter sophistication?"

Her thin body tensed. "I don't know what you're referring to. I suggest that you never repeat that lie to anyone else."

In our world it's usually the lie that becomes the truth. That's because we don't call it a lie. We call it hype. And hype in our world is morality-free. But I had to give Monique credit at how quickly and brazenly she had turned the truth into a lie. That's just pure power.

"I guess I'll be looking for another agent," I said.

"Good luck." She didn't mean it. She slammed the door on her way out.

I sat down in the blue slipper chair and faced the mirror. Well, I just blew another connection. I gave my reflection a congratulatory smile. There was some wine left in the bottle, but no glass. I took a drink and stared at the gown.

So Kyra didn't wear it. She had defied her mother. Maybe there was hope, I thought, as I watched a pink ruffle edging the hem of the gown change color. I peered closer. It turned a deeper pink. Then it turned red. The red color grew darker and began to glisten as it oozed free of the hem forming a small rivulet of blood on the blue wool carpet. I lifted up the skirt. Jimmy Whitelaw was curled into a fetal position. Blood matted the front of his expensive white shirt. His once cocky eyes were now a cloudy blue. I let the skirt flutter back down over him. Maybe Kyra had more than defied her mother.

Had I just experienced a sense of hope? What had it felt like? I couldn't remember.

I walked out of the bedroom and out the front door of the house. I asked the valet if he had my car.

"Oh, sorry. What kind was it?'

"Old green Jag."

He disappeared in the darkness quickly returning with it. I drove away.

I stopped at the Ralph's Market in Hollywood to pick up some milk and coffee. I needed them. But I needed to do something normal and mundane even more. I had just witnessed a mother selling off her daughter. I had just discovered the dead body of Jimmy Whitelaw. And what did I do? Leave the party. Oh, Diana.

My hands shook as I ground my mocha java beans. I recognized an actress that I had recently met. We had both been up for a dog food commercial. Neither one of us had got it. I attempted a smile but it wasn't in me. And she looked as if I had discovered her doing something she shouldn't have been doing. As if being alone in a market at night picking up a few normal, mundane things to keep her sad lonely life together wasn't something I should see. Avoiding me, she ducked down another aisle.

I paid the cashier and walked back to my car. As I put the grocery bag in the back seat I noticed my trunk was ajar. I opened it and looked in. Nothing but a flat spare tire and a pink barrette. I picked up the barrette. It was the same one Monique had fastened in her daughter's hair.

I ran through the parking lot out to the sidewalk. As I looked up the street the lights of the oncoming cars momentarily blinded me. Then I saw Kyra. She was sitting on a bus bench wearing a wool cap pulled low. There was no mistaking her up-turned nose and pointed chin. I sat down next to her.

"Go away, Diana. I'm not going home."

"You forgot your barrette. What if I hadn't stopped here but drove all the way to Malibu? What would you have done?"

"Hitched my way up the coast. He tried to rape me. I'm not a virgin but that doesn't mean I have to allow myself to be raped. Even for my mother. He had his arm on my throat and every time I lifted my head I choked. I felt the gun in his pocket. I didn't even think. I just took it and shot. I hated him. I hate my mother."

Tears glistened on her cheeks. I tried to put my arm around.

She stiffened at my touch. "I just stood there waiting for people to run up to my bedroom because of the noise the gun made, but nobody did. I guess that fake rap band my mother hired was too loud. I couldn't look at Jimmy's body. I put that stupid gown over him. Then I got dressed and went downstairs and wandered through the party. I really didn't know that many people. Except that they were famous. I saw you talking to a man. You looked happy, Diana. Everyone looked like they were having a good time. Then I walked down our driveway until I saw your car. I tried the trunk, it was open, and I got in." She snuffed back more tears.

"Come with me and tell the police that."

"Are you kidding? I'll have to tell them that mother set the whole thing up. I can't to that."

"Why? I was there. I'll vouch for you."

"Will you really, Diana?" Teenage sarcasm and distrust riddled her voice. "You can trust me."

"I don't think so."

We watched the cars race past us. When the light changed red the cars screeched to a stop inches from one another as if jockeying for a minute piece of space kept them all in the unnamed race.

"You said you used his gun. What did you do with it?" I asked.

She gazed at the nylon duffle bag on her lap. "I need it for protection."

"Jimmy can't hurt you anymore. At least let me take the gun."

"No!" She edged away from me. "How often do the buses come by?" she asked, nervously. "I've never taken one." She gripped a twenty-dollar bill in her hand.

"I took buses when I was a teenager. Kyra, I don't think bus drivers make change anymore."

"He will for me." For a moment she sounded like her mother.

"But they don't carry change."

"When you took the bus as a teenager where were you going?"

"I had a job in downtown L.A. I was a fitter's model."

"Then you knew where you were going."

"Let's say I had a destination. Kyra please let me take you home. Whatever your mother may have done, she wants to know you're okay."

"Then tell her I'm okay. Also tell her I have a gun."

"Why do you want me to tell her that?"

She peered at me in the shadowy light. "How can you be old and so naive?"

A bus pulled up: its airbrakes made a loud swooshing sound. Its interior was lit up like an all night Denny's Restaurant. We watched the working poor and the illegal aliens straggle off.

"Good-bye, Diana."

I grabbed her arm. She wrenched away and leaped up the steps of the bus. The door clamped shut. It pulled out into traffic. I could see her standing, swaying, talking to the driver. I was sure he would pull over and make her get off. But he didn't. Then she was talking to a passenger who began to make change for her. Just like her mother, she could talk anybody into anything. It was then I realized I hadn't got the destination of the bus or its number.

Two hours later I was drinking a glass of wine on the rotting wood balcony of my Malibu teardown. Next-door Ryan Johns' house, separated by a narrow path from mine, towered in wealth and importance. I heard Ryan staggering up the steps to his stone balcony.

Swaying he grabbed the newel post and yelled at me, "You're a bitter lonely woman, Diana Poole."

"And you're a drunken hack," I yelled back.

This had somehow become our usual greeting.

"Why do you hate me?" he asked.

Ryan Johns was a man who would betray his friends for connections. A man who stayed sober long enough to write what the movie stars and the money people wanted him to write. Then he'd hit the bottle, turning his self-loathing into drunken charm. Did I say betray his friends for his connections? Had I betrayed Kyra? If I had gone to help her sooner maybe I could have prevented Whitelaw's death and kept a young girl from destroying her life.

"I don't hate you, Ryan."

I went into the house and closed the sliding glass door. I stared at my husband's two Oscars on the fireplace mantle. He had won them for Best Screenwriter on two different movies. They were the only tangible evidence of his life that he had left me besides this house I could no longer afford. We had lived too well, never thinking of the future, or of death. I should wrap them in newspaper and put them in a box, I thought. It was time. And then I felt that deep ache for the need of his arms around me.

The doorbell rang. I answered it. It was Detective Heath. His attitude was causal and threatening at the same time. His charming smile had disappeared.

"According to Monique Lancer you were the last person she saw in Kyra's bedroom. That is except for when she discovered Jimmy Whitelaw's body."

"Would you like to come in?"

He followed me into the living room.

"I take it by your composed reaction to my news that you knew Whitelaw was dead. Did you know Kyra is missing, too?"

"Yes and yes." I sat on the sofa. He remained standing, legs apart, hands jammed into his pant pockets.

"But I'm calm only because a certain amount of time has passed."

"Good. I wouldn't want to upset you. Though I could get technical and say you left a murder scene."

"Are you going to?"

"It depends on what you tell me."

I described how I had discovered Whitelaw's body and then he asked: "So where is Kyra?"

"I'm getting to that. On my way home from the party ..."

"This is after discovering Whitelaw's body?"

"Yes. I stopped at Ralph's market in Hollywood. I bought milk and coffee."

"You always do grocery shopping after discovering a dead body? What's with you people?"

"Do you want to hear what I have to say or not?"

"Go on."

I told him how I had found my trunk open, the barrette, and then Kyra on the bus bench.

"What bus was she taking?"

"I didn't get the number or the destination."

"She could be anywhere. I'd like to think that you didn't help her."

"If she had taken a chance on me I probably would have. But she didn't. She thought I depended on her mother."

"For what?"

"Any small parts she could toss my way."

"How did you know to look under the evening gown?"

"I saw the blood seeping through the fabric. I lifted the hem and there he was. I put it back down and got in my car."

"With Kyra in the trunk."

"Except I didn't know she was in my trunk."

"Monique Lancer said that Jimmy Whitelaw went up to her daughter's room to escort her down to the party."

"That's not true. I was there. Monique wanted Kyra to have sex with him. Monique thought that would get him to take her on as his agent."

"By pimping her daughter? What is it with you people?"

"That's the second time you've asked that. Do you really expect an answer?"

He looked at me for a long a moment then said, "Someday, but not now."

"By the way, Monique will deny what I just told you. And there's something else. Kyra told me Whitelaw got rough with her. That it was really a rape. From what little I know of him I believe her story."

"Whitelaw was shot."

"I know."

"Kyra confessed to you, didn't she?"

I nodded. Tears ran down my cheeks. He awkwardly and briskly reached into his pocket and handed me his handkerchief. It smelled of Shalimar.

"Who wears Shalimar?"

"Third ex-wife. Where did Kyra get the gun?"

"She said Jimmy had it in his pocket."

"We can't find it. Does Kyra have it?"

His dark eyes burrowed into me. I was afraid if the police knew she was armed they'd hurt her.

"I don't know," I answered.

"For an actress you're not a very good liar. What time was it when she got on the bus?"

"I'm not sure. I left the party around eight thirty. Between 9:30 and ten. I'm only guessing."

He reached in his pocket for his cell phone. When he made his connection he snapped out orders to check the bus schedules for the time and the area. Then he added that Kyra might be armed.

"I didn't say she had a gun."

"I didn't either. Why didn't you phone the police after she got on the bus?"

"There was a moment at the party. I was standing on the stairs and watched Whitelaw go into Krya's room. I didn't do anything to stop it. Her mother and I should be held accountable. Not Kyra." My tears started again.

He slipped the phone back in his pocket. "Doesn't work that way."

He stood in front of the Oscars.

"Did you win these?"

"My husband was Colin Hudson. They're his."

"You were married to Colin Hudson? God, he was a great writer. The Paddy Chayevsky of our time. How long ago did he die, if you don't mind me asking?"

"A little over a year. You want to pick one up, don't you?" I said.

"Do you mind?"

"No."

"Heavy." He weighed the Oscar in his hands and grinned sheepishly. "I suppose everybody says that."

"Take it."

"What?"

"Take it home with you."

"Is this some kind of bribe?"

"I'm trying to let go. Besides I thought it might help with your writer's block. Or maybe understand what kind of people we are."

"You're trying to let go of your husband?"

"I think it's about time."

"Well if I were you I wouldn't start with giving away his Oscars. I'd do something a little more practical."

"Such as?"

"Find another man." He looked quickly away from me and returned the statuette to its place on the mantel. "Here's my card. It has my cell phone number on it. If Kyra calls you, or you remember anything else I want you to call me. Understand?"

"Yes. Here's your handkerchief."

"Keep it."

"No thanks. I hate the smell of Shalimar."

"So do I. It's suffocating." He threw it into the fireplace. "See how easy it is to let go?"

"You must know. Three ex-wives. "

I placed his card on my nightstand. I took a sleeping pill and went to bed.

At two in the morning the phone jarred me out of my sleep.

"Diana?"

"Yes?"

"It's Kyra."

I sat up pulling the covers around me. "Are you all right?"

"I'm going to do the only thing I can. The only thing that will really hurt my mother."

"What are you going to do?"

"What I should have done. You'll be reading about it."

"Where are you, Kyra? Please let me help you."

She hung up.

I thought of calling Monique. To warn her. But of what? I didn't believe Kyra would physically harm her mother. I got up and put on jeans and a sweater, and made myself coffee. At four-thirty the phone rang again. It was Monique.

"I'm in my car on the way to your house. Kyra called. She wants me to pick her up. She wants you to be there too."

"Where?"

"Near the restaurant at Paradise Cove. I'll be at your house in about twenty minutes." She hung up. Like a true agent she didn't wait for my answer.

I called Leo Heath. He answered groggily.

"If I tell you something about Kyra you have to promise me you won't show up with an army of cops."

He agreed and I told him that Monique and I were going to pick her up. I didn't trust him enough to tell him that Kyra had told me she wanted to hurt her mother.

"I'll follow you there," he said. "Monique doesn't have to know."

"But she's going to be here soon."

"I'm just down the street from you."

"You live in this area?"

"No. I'm sleeping in my car. My third wife tossed me out yesterday. I haven't had time to find a place."

"Are you watching my house?"

"Now how can I do that when I've been asleep?"

Monique picked me up and we drove up the coast. Paradise Cove wasn't far from where I lived.

"How did Kyra get to the cove?" I asked.

"Hitchhiked from Santa Monica."

"I wonder why she didn't get dropped off at my house?"

"Maybe she thought you'd call the police."

I tried not to turn around and see if Heath was behind us; but since I didn't know what kind of car he drove I wouldn't be able to tell anyway.

"What are you going to do?" I asked her.

"Our lawyer said I'm to take her to him. He would arrange with the police to bring her in. What have I done, Diana?"

I didn't respond.

"I just thought that if she'd given herself to all those creeps why couldn't she give herself to someone who could help us? I don't know where the boundaries are anymore. Where the lines are drawn. It just seemed that nothing meant anything to her. So why would Jimmy?"

"Kyra called me."

"When?"

"Around two this morning?"

"What did she say?"

"She said she wanted to hurt you."

"What does that mean?" Her hands tightened on the steering wheel.

"I don't know. What did she say to you when she called you to pick her up?"

"Nothing. Just that she wanted to turn herself in."

"When I talked to her earlier she implied she had the gun to protect her against you."

"Does she truly believe I would physically harm her? Oh God, Diana, what have I done?"

We drove in silence. There was a heavy wet mist and we seemed to be the only people on the Pacific Coast Highway.

"She has a gun, Diana. I'm scared of my own daughter."

"But you said she wanted me to come along. She's not going to harm you if I'm there. Kyra is not a cold-blooded killer."

Tears showed on Monique's face. They looked out of place. I remembered Kyra's tears as we sat on the bus bench.

"Did you ever want to be a mother, Diana?"

"I was more interested in being loved myself."

"By Colin?"

"Yes."

"I was more interested in my career. But I thought I could have it all. Women always get screwed."

I was so tired of hearing women say this. We repeated, 'I thought we could have it all,' like a mantra of self-torture, constantly reminding us of what we hadn't gained. Or if we had, it was tainted by what we had to give up. Why did women think they could escape loss?

As we sped closer to our destination, I said, "My first modeling job was a fashion layout for bathing suits. We shot it at Paradise Cove. I remember I glued fake plastic nails over my stubby ones. They had a live trained seal they wanted me to pose with. He swayed his big head and hit my hand. All my nails flew off. I was mortified."

"Is there a moral to this, Diana?"

"I was Kyra's age. Sixteen. I was still a virgin. And I was worried about plastic nails."

"Different time."

"Now we have acrylic nails and no virgins. Do you love your daughter?"

"Of course." She said matter-of-factly. And I felt chill.

Turning left, Monique guided the Mercedes down a steep road into the cove and the restaurant's empty parking lot. I looked in my side view mirror. I thought I could make out the shadow of another car behind us. The Mercedes' lights pierced the mist. I put the window down. The sound of the ocean crashing against the shore and the thick damp salty air filled the car. My heart pounded.

"Do you see her?" Monique asked breathlessly.

"No. Drive slower."

"Oh, Diana," she murmured. "I'm afraid of her. Afraid of my own daughter. You talk to her. I can't."

"Stop!"

She slammed her foot on the break. We both lurched forward as the car skidded to a stop.

"Did you see something? Hear something?" Monique asked breathlessly.

I peered out the window.

"Is it Kyra?" Monique asked.

I opened the car door. With the car's headlights as a guide I slowly approached what appeared to be a bundle of clothes on the asphalt. But my gut knew it wasn't just clothes. It was Kyra. She was curled in the same fetal position as Jimmy Whitelaw had been. The right side of her head had a bloody hole in it. A gun rested near her hand. Monique got out of the car.

"Kyra? Kyra!"

"Stop her!

Confused, I turned and saw Heath running toward us yelling, "Stop her!"

Monique fell to her knees and pulled Kyra's body to hers. She began to rock her, and sob. I stepped back and felt Heath standing behind me. Trembling I wondered if this was what Kyra had meant about hurting her mother.

Heath rested his hand on my shoulder for a moment.

"Stop her from what?" I asked.

Instead of answering he impassively studied a mother holding her dead daughter. He looked like a director who was unable to get the scene to work right.

"Evidence. Contaminated now," he said to no one in particular.

Kyra's death was declared a suicide. Hollywood closed ranks around Monique Lancer. Her client list might be aging, but she still had power. The rumor that she had prostituted her own daughter was said to be scurrilous and spread by those who had personal axes to grind. And the hot new Jimmy Whitelaw was quickly forgotten. His unfinished movie was dumped along with my ten lines and one close-up. But the image of Kyra huddled in death on the cold asphalt of the parking lot never left me. I couldn't forget her telling me that the gun was for her own protection. And then there were Heath's words: *contaminated evidence.*

A few days later I called him and asked him out to dinner. We met at a restaurant near my house.

"Are we on a date?" he asked, as we sipped our drinks.

"No. I mean I hadn't thought of it that way."

"You want something. What?"

"I'm a woman who lives a chaotic life and I would like to tie up some lose ends."

"I like tying up lose ends. Are you sure we're not on a date?"

"I think Monique killed her daughter. I also think she wanted me to be a witness."

He sat back. "You mean Monique wanted you to see her discovering the daughter she had just murdered. But Kyra said she wanted to hurt her mother. Wouldn't suicide do that?"

"It would hurt Monique more if she came back home. If she told the truth."

"About her trying to prostitute Kyra."

"Yes. Right now it's just a rumor. Hollywood can deal with that. It's the truth we have trouble with."

"So you're saying what?"

"I think Kyra called to have her mother pick her up. I think Monique went to Paradise Cove and shot her with the gun Kyra had. Then called me. Remember she was only twenty minutes away when she called. About the time it takes to get from the cove to my house."

"And what proof do you have for all this?"

"You said it. She contaminated the evidence by holding Kyra to her own body."

"That's not proof. To a jury that's a mother grieving."

"You're a detective. Doesn't it bother you that she could get away with this?"

"People do get away with murder, Diana."

"I guess my only hope is that she gets drunk one night and the booze and the guilt get the best of her and she confesses."

He studied me for moment then said, "There is one thing Monique Lancer could do that would at least let you know she did it."

"What?"

"Take you on as a client."

"What would that prove?"

"You're the one who knows for sure she was using Kyra to get Jimmy Whitelaw. If she did kill her daughter she'd be even more worried about you. But taking you on as a client would give her control over you. Make you hers. Ease her worries."

A loud noise came from the bar area as a man fell off his bar stool. Two waiters picked him up. It was Ryan Johns. As they dragged him out of the restaurant he spotted me and yelled, "Diana, you're a lonely bitter woman."

The diners peered at me. There was a ripple of laughter. Heath raised his eyebrows.

"Ryan Johns. He lives next door," I tried to explain.

"Are you a lonely bitter woman, Diana?" Intimacy warmed his voice.

"Are you a lonely bitter man?"

We leaned closer, our lips touching. I took Leo Heath home that night. I let myself experience the warmth and passion of another man in my bed

When I got up late the next morning he was gone. There was no note. In the kitchen I checked my voice mail. He had left a message.

"I had an early meeting. I didn't want to wake you. I thought of writing you a note but I have writer's block. I'll call you in a little while." I smiled as he hung up.

I had a second message. I heard Monique Lancer's voice. She asked me to come on board. To be her client. After all, we had been through so much together. How could she not extend to me? "I'll call again. We need each other, Diana," she added then hung up.

My skin turned cold.

I took my coffee and stood on my deck and breathed in the morning air and thought of Kyra and me sitting on the bus bench together. I had let her go. I should have held on to her tight. You only have such a short time to hold onto the living.

Someone yawned loudly. I peered over the rail. Ryan Johns was passed out on the walkway. I put my coffee down and grabbed the hose that was curled in the corner and turned it on full force. I aimed it at him. He jolted up shaking like a bear.

"Jesus Christ, Diana."

"I'm not a bitter woman."

"What?" he staggered to his feet.

"Lonely. And very, very sad. But I'm not bitter."

"Does that mean I'm not a hack?"

"No!" I went into the living room.

The phone was ringing.

This is a story about my fascination with women in Hollywood who look for their self-esteem in mirrors, in the camera, and especially in a man's eyes. And how far some women will go to protect their own lack of self-worth.

WHAT'S IT WORTH?

Emma Parker had left her keys in her front door. Since I was meeting her for lunch I used them to let myself in. I found her in the living room. Wearing a faded blue chenille bath robe, she was on her hands and knees, peering under the sofa. The sofa looked like it came right out of a forties movie with its big green-leaf print fabric. I imagined Eve Arden and Joan Crawford sitting on it, sharing snappy dialogue.

"What are you looking for?" I asked.

She peered over her shoulder at me. A thick strand of henna-colored hair flopped across her check. "My self-worth." Emma was an actress. "And those." Her tired green eyes focused on the keys dangling from my hand.

"You left them in the front door," I explained.

Staying on the floor she leaned her back against the couch. "Oh, man, I'm such a mess, Diana. We were supposed to have lunch weren't we?"

"You wanted to talk about Lund? I think you referred to him as that son-of- a-bitch director who fired you." I set the keys on the coffee table.

Emma and I had both read for the part of Livonia in Lund Hagan's movie. Despite the character's exotic name it was the typical dutiful wife role which means there is very little dialogue and the actress stands around looking loving, worried, and makes a lot coffee. But the movie was directed by Hagan, who was known for his taste and intelligence.

A rare commodity in Hollywood. He was also known for being a narcissistic bastard who was difficult to work with. Not a rare commodity in Hollywood. Emma got the part. Two days into shooting Lund Hagan had fired her. This is the kind of blow to an actress' career and ego that makes waitressing look good.

"Oh, God, I'm so hung over." Emma held her head in her hands. Then she anxiously peered up at me. "Do you mind if we don't have lunch? I'm not feeling well."

"No, of course not. Can I get you anything?"

As she struggled to her feet the bedroom door opened, and Lund Hagan sauntered in buttoning his black shirt. His black leather jacket was slung over his arm. At least his jeans were zipped up. The director was a tall aloofly handsome man in his early fifties with thick blonde hair fading to white. His blue eyes were as warm as two ice cubes. Right now he had the conceited look of having just signed a multi-million dollar contract, or a having had great night in bed. It was hard to tell which. These expressions can be interchangeable in Hollywood.

"Diana Poole," he said, surprised. We shook hands awkwardly.

"I was just on my way out," I said.

"On your way out?" he repeated, smiling haughtily. "You should never say that in Hollywood. It might come true. You won't tell anyone that you saw me here, will you?" He meant his wife, the producer of his films, and his mistress, the biggest casting director in town.

"This is so embarrassing." Emma slumped onto the sofa.

Ignoring Lund, I said, "I'll talk to you later, Emma."

"I'm sorry, Diana," I heard her say as I left the house.

In my car I wondered why Emma had gone to bed with Lund Hagan. Surely she didn't think she'd get her part back. I looked at my watch. I had a call-back for a TV commercial at two-thirty. So I had a couple of hours to kill. I decided to go to Saks and buy moisturizer. It was all I could afford.

My husband, Colin, died suddenly of a heart attack about a year ago and left me with no life insurance. He did leave me with our house – now referred to by the realtors as a tear-down – in Malibu; an old green Jag that blew hot air from its vents no matter what the weather was; and two Oscars. Colin had won each for Best Screenplay. He also left me with an empty spot where my heart should be. I had been an actress before I married Colin, and now I'd gone back to acting in an attempt to keep the life that he and I had loved. Of course I was older now and the competition for my kind of role was brutal.

Standing at the make-up counter in Saks I looked at my reflection in the counter mirror and wondered why they always tilted these things so you saw your neck, chin, and nostrils. My hair was determinedly blonde and my eyes blue. A pretty face that was becoming more set in its ways. Less optimistic. Less adaptable. Again I thought of Emma. Maybe she did think she'd get her part back. Desperation can do that to you.

Completing my purchase, I let the escalator drift me upstairs. With my little Saks bag in hand, I wandered around staring at the expensively dressed mannequins. I became aware of other females roaming and looking. Did they just have time on their hands? Or were they Madame Bovarys searching for that perfect dress for the perfect romantic lover? The perfect romantic dream.

It was then I saw Carol Hagan, Lund's wife. She was with Val Franz, his mistress. A saleslady was ushering them toward the dressing rooms. They were the last two women on earth I wanted to encounter. I ducked behind a tall rack of evening gowns, hiding as if I'd done something wrong. While being slashed by sequins, I tried to figure out the implications of a wife and mistress shopping together. When did sequins make a comeback?

"Diana?" Carol's voice cut through the cushy silence. She swiftly parted the hangers on the rack like a female Moses parting the Red Sea.

"Are you hiding from us?" Val, the mistress asked with wry smile.

They carried large expensive purses slung over their shoulders. The bags were so big they looked as if they needed bellboys to carry them. Each woman held an iPhone.

"Carol. Val. Of course not." I grabbed a gown and held it up to me.

"That's a size two," Val said dryly, placing a hand on her sharp bony hip. Val was a size two. Her dark hair was pulled back from her lean carved face. Physically she appeared to be all edges, but her personality was cautious, even thoughtful.

"It looks like something a drag queen would wear," Carol, the wife, grabbed the dress from me and threw it on a low-slung leather chair. Her hair was a mass of graying curls. She had all the personality and subtly of a John Deere tractor. Lund was a man of divergent taste in women.

"Why are you avoiding us?" Carol persisted.

"Haven't you ever wanted to be alone?"

"Not in Saks." Val smiled.

"This is déjà vu that we've run into you," Carol said.

"Serendipity," Val corrected her.

"We were going to call you, but we can't get a hold of Lund." Carol shook her iPhone as if to make it ring. "Did you hear that Emma Parker's off the movie?"

"Yes."

"I told Lund she was wrong for the part. Too neurotic. Too New Yorky. But he had a vision." She paused, her lips curved down. "He didn't come home last night, and he wasn't with Val ..." Her voice quivered then trailed off.

"You were on the short list for the role, Diana," Val continued for her.

They were like a married couple correcting each other and picking up the other's train of thought.

"We need to talk now." Carol had regained her composure.

The two women guided me to a private dressing room and promptly dismissed the saleslady. I sat on a sofa. My tiny Saks bag looked pathetic in this room filled with Charles Chang Lima outfits and Prada suits. My reflection was on display in the three way mirror. I wore jeans and a crisp white shirt. I felt fleshy and all breasts compared to these two women.

They began to undress. Val had the body of a mistress, toned and exercised. Carol had the body of a wife, thin but sagging.

"I was trying to reach Lund to set up a meeting for you." Carol stepped into a pair of blue-and-white striped trousers. "He told me he was going to sleep at the office. Why does he lie?" she asked Val.

Val shimmied into a black dress. "He can't help himself. Even when he doesn't need to lie, he lies. Diana, we'll set up a meeting with you and Lund later today. It'll just be perfunctory. There isn't time to interview other actresses, and he knows it."

"Let me get this straight. You're offering me the role of the wife in Lund's movie?"

"Yes," they said in unison.

I had a jolt of pure optimism; the kind that shoots through an actor when she hears the word 'yes'. It felt as if I'd just downed a Starbuck's espresso laced with steroids. I was keenly alert and able to do anything, especially have a career. Then I thought of Lund sauntering out of Emma Parker's bedroom and my optimism ebbed.

"His secretary didn't know where he was," Carol snapped angrily. "For God's sake, the movie is shut down. My ass is on the line." She stared at her ass in the mirror then zipped Val up. In return Val held up a blue-and-white pinstripe jacket for Carol to slip into.

"Maybe Lund doesn't want me for the role? I did read for him. He didn't seem impressed," I said.

"Lund needs to be pushed into a corner," Val said.

"It's the only way he can make a decision," Carol explained.

"So we're pushing." Val studied her reflection. "A little black dress. Perfect for a funeral. There's always one or two a year at least." Now her gaze was on me. "We always wanted you for the part of the wife. You have that genteel suburban look. All the other actresses we've seen look like they're trying out for *The Wives of Orange County*."

Val grabbed her iPhone off a chair and answered, "Yes?"

It must've made a noise that only dogs and Val could hear because I hadn't heard anything. She began talking about another movie she was casting.

Carol grabbed her iPhone and punched something, then snapped, "Is he back yet? Get him now."

I sat staring at my little Saks bag feeling doomed and exhilarated at the same time when my cell phone rang. I fumbled around in my purse, finally digging it out and answering it.

"He's gone. Diana, I just want to say again that I'm sorry about forgetting our lunch." It was Emma.

"Listen don't worry about it ... I can't talk right now."

"One more thing. Lund was so sweet when he told me I hadn't worked out for the part. He said let's get a drink. One thing led to another. Somehow I thought if I went to bed with him he'd give me back the role. A sort of reversal of the casting couch seduction. Screw the director after you lost the part."

"Where the hell have you been, Lund?" Carol snarled into her cell.

"Where are you?" Emma asked me

"I'm on a call-back for Herbal Heart. I have to go."

"You know what's really sick? I think I'm falling for him." Emma hung up.

"Four o'clock, Lund." Carol disconnected her phone and looked at me. "The meeting is set."

"Does he know it's me he's seeing?" I asked.

"Of course he does. What's wrong with you, Diana?"

"I'm not sure."

Val was off her phone now and studying me. "What's Herbal Heart?"

"I've got a call back for a commercial for a premenopausal pill. It's called Herbal Heart."

Carol stepped out of her pinstripe trousers. "I look like a two-bit gangster in this suit." She turned on me. "Did you say premenopausal pill? Hawking anything that has to do with a woman aging is a bad career move for you, Diana. Don't do it."

"Who were you talking too?" Val smiled slyly. "Why did you lie about being on a call-back and not here with us?"

"I was talking to somebody who wouldn't understand ... I should go on this commercial. You know, just in case." I stood.

"You're going to get this part in Lund's movie, Diana, if I have to stuff you down his throat. So don't bother with that other shit. And don't forget four o'clock. Lund's office." Carol was now bare legged, wearing only the gangster like pinstripe jacket. She looked like an aged chorus girl searching for a production of *Guys and Dolls*.

You need to have a career in order to make a bad career move. So I did go to the call-back for Herbal Heart. I was playing a wife in that one too. Herbal Heart was going to make me a whole woman again so I could enjoy playing with my Labrador and my husband. The director and client smiled and nodded and said they'd let me know.

At four o'clock I was sitting in Lund Hagan's office.

Like many directors' offices, Lund's had a rented, transitory feeling to it. It was large enough to be impressive as was his leather chair and glass- and-metal desk. The only personal touches were a couple of posters from his most recent movies and a Best Director Oscar sitting on a dull gray filing cabinet.

Lund's cold eyes took me in. "I see you, Val, and Carol have been very busy. What did you tell them?" He rose from his chair, forcing me to look up at him.

"Nothing."

"You expect me to believe that?" He came around and sat on the edge of his desk and scratched his perfectly unshaven chin. "Let's put our cards on the table, Diana. If I don't hire you, you're going to tell them about Emma and me. Isn't that how it works?"

"No."

"You expect me to believe that?"

"Yes."

"You were on Val's and Carol's short list. Not mine. I never took you for a player, Diana."

By player he meant a conniver and schemer.

"Do you want me for this role or not? I have a long drive back to Malibu."

"You've pushed me into a corner. I have no choice." He put up his hands like a man being held at gun point.

I thought of the money I would earn and the prestige this role could bring me. I thought of my rotting wood deck, leaky roof, and my Jag's heater that never turned off. What difference did it make if Lund Hagan thought I was blackmailing him?

"I'll do my best for you, Lund," I heard myself say.

"I'll make you look damn good on film, Diana. But if Carol or Val hear one word about Emma and me, I can make you look just as bad, or reduce your part to nothing in the editing room."

I drove to Malibu with the setting sun in my eyes.

At one o'clock in the morning the phone rang pulling me out of a restless sleep.

"How could you do this, Diana!" Emma Parker screamed at me.

"Do what?"

"I looked up to you. You and Colin were the golden couple because you both had principle!"

"Are we talking about the role of the wife?"

"Yes! You are the last person I ever thought would use blackmail to get ..."

"I'm not blackmailing anyone."

"You threatened to tell Val and Carol if Lund didn't give you the part."

"Did he tell you that? It's not true. I was on the short list. Val and Carol got me a meeting with Lund. It had nothing to do with you and him."

"Really? And how did you get to see Val and Carol?"

I told her what had happened at Saks.

There was a long heavy pause, then, "You expect me to believe that Carol and Val were sharing a dressing room in Saks and invited you in to give you the role of the wife?"

"Yes."

"When was this?"

"After I left you."

"So you were with them in a dressing room at Saks when I called you?"

"Yes."

"No you weren't. You were on the call back for Herbal Heart. You should get your lies straight, Diana." She slammed the phone down.

On the set four days later, I was pouring coffee into a mug. It was cold. But I blew on it as if it were hot. Sense memory. I listened to Josh Black, the actor, tell me there was nothing wrong with our married life. Beyond the lights voices were raised from the shadowy sound stage. Josh continued his lines but without conviction until Lund yelled, "Cut, God damn't!" Then, confronting two men in suits, he fumed, "I'm shooting a movie here."

The makeup woman rushed onto the set and began dabbing at my face. "Did you hear?" she said in a low voice. "Emma Parker was murdered."

"What?" I slumped against the fake kitchen counter. "I can't believe it."

The set lights dimmed. Now I could see the people on the soundstage clearly. The taller of the two men talking to Lund turned in my direction. I sucked in my breath. It was Detective Leo Heath. His dark hair was cut short and graying at the temples. His dark intelligent eyes turned hard as he took me in. The last time I saw him was in my bed. In my arms. He had left early in the morning. But he had called. He had left messages. I never returned any of them.

The next day, Friday, *Variety* ran a headline: AXED ACTRESS SHOT DEAD. On Saturday I sat on my deck hiding my face from the sun under a battered straw hat. The police had questioned Lund, but when they narrowed down the time of Emma's death he had an alibi. He was with his mistress and his wife. I was waiting to be questioned.

"Do you have an alibi?" Ryan Johns, my next-door neighbor, sprawled on my lounge. His house, oozing money and success, towered over mine. He wore Bermuda shorts, a Hawaiian shirt, a gold Piaget watch, and Ugg boots.

"I was here. Alone. I haven't been questioned."

"You could say you were with me." He belched then leered at me. He was on his fifth Corona.

"Do you really think I need an alibi?"

His bleary blue eyes took me in. Then he shook his head causing his red curly hair to bounce like springs. "This is Hollywood, Diana. They're going to need a suspect and quickly. Do you think Lund hasn't told the police you were blackmailing him?"

"But I wasn't. Val and Carol know that."

"Let me be your alibi, Diana. Let me do something for you." He sat up and stared out over the railing.

I lifted my hat and followed his gaze. Detective Leo Heath stood on the beach looking up at us. His hands were in his pant pockets. The breeze bellowed his jacket out and blew his tie over his shoulder. Sunglasses covered his eyes. Then he reached into his pocket and showed his badge, as if I didn't know he was the police. It caught the sun and glimmered. Then he pointed at the locked gate that led from the beach to the pathway that separated my house from Ryan's. I got up and let him in.

When we were back on the deck, I said, "I have a front door." I sounded cold and aloof and immediately regretted my tone.

"You didn't answer it. Your Jag was in the car port so I came around the long way." He looked at Ryan.

"Who are you?" He slipped ofF his glasses and rubbed the bridge of his pugilistic nose.

"Ryan Johns. I live next door."

Leo nodded as he stamped his feet trying to knock the sand off his shoes. Then his smile slid sideways. "Nice outfit. You in the biz?"

"Screenwriter."

He turned back to me. "Wasn't your husband a screenwriter?" He knew damn well he was.

"Yes."

He nodded vaguely. "I have some questions I'd like to ask you, Miss Poole."

We went into the living room. I demanded that Ryan stay. I needed a buffer between me and Leo Heath. Ryan and I sat on the sofa. I took off my hat and ran my hand through my hair. Heath stood by the fireplace. Colin's Oscars glimmered from the mantel.

"What is it you would like to ask me?" I asked.

"When was the last time you saw Emma Parker?"

I told him about going to her house but paused, remembering Lund coming out of the bedroom.

"Anybody else there?"

I related my encounter with Lund.

He nodded. "Then where did you go?"

I told him about running into Val and Carol at Saks and how they offered me the role of The Wife in the dressing room.

"Is that about the time Emma called you? I have her list of calls from her cell phone."

I explained the awkwardness of the phone call.

"So you lied to her."

"It wasn't exactly a lie. How did you know?"

"Val Franz, the mistress, said you told whoever you were taking to that you were on an Herbal Heart call-back."

"What's that?" Ryan asked between gulps of his Corona.

"A natural hormone for early menopause," I snapped.

He gaped at me. "Oh, Diana, that's a bad career move."

"Could we get back to why you lied to Emma Parker?" Leo asked dryly.

"I couldn't very well tell her I was with Lund's wife and mistress. I mean she had just gone to bed with him. Nor could I tell her that I was being offered the part that she had just been fired from."

"By the man she had just gone to bed with," he said in a tired voice. Then his dark eyes bore into me. "Why not?"

"Because she was in a delicate state and I didn't have time to explain and I didn't want Val and Carol to know Lund was with Emma."

"Confusing, isn't it?" Ryan observed.

"No. It's stupid."

I felt as if I had to defend Emma. Or was it me? "This from a man with three wives?" I blurted.

Ryan stared at Leo then at me. Leo ignored the comment by looking at his notes.

"Emma Parker was killed between one and three in the morning on Tuesday. Where were you at that time?"

"She was with me," Ryan announced too quickly, like an actor rushing his cue.

Leo smiled crookedly. "Were you dressed like that when she was with you?"

Ryan slammed his beer onto the table and stood. "She's not saying any more."

"Ryan." I took his hand and pulled him back down to the sofa.

Leo turned to study the statuettes on the mantel. "I see you didn't get rid of Colin's Oscars. Weren't you going to do that?"

"I was trying to let go."

He swung around facing me. "But just for one night."

"What is that suppose to mean?!"

"My God! You went to bed with him." Ryan stared at me accusingly. "I can see it on your face and his. You both look pathetic."

"This coming from a guy wearing Uggs," Leo snorted.

"It was a mistake, Ryan."

"A cop? You went to bed with a cop? You're an actress, an artist. How could you go to bed with a cop? And not me?"

"So were you still with her from one to three o'clock in the morning?" Leo asked.

Before Ryan was forced to answer, I said, "No he wasn't. I was here in bed. Alone. Who has an alibi for those hours anyway?"

"Some people do."

"Well maybe they need to have one."

"I would just like to say one thing, Diana." Ryan was now at the sliding doors facing us. "When the great screenwriter, Herman Mankiewicz, drunkenly threw up on the table during a dinner party at Hearst's castle, he turned to his hostess, Marion Davis, and said, 'Don't worry, Marion, the white wine went with the fish.' Think about it." He opened the door and left.

"What does that mean, and why do you have to think about it?" Leo asked.

"Maybe it means you can get away with anything as long as the white wine goes with the fish," I said.

"Is that why you didn't call me back? We don't go together?"

"You were divorcing your third wife and I'm still mourning my husband. That's not a great combination."

"You may need a lawyer."

"Why?"

"Lund Hagan said you were blackmailing him to get Emma Parker's role. Val Franz and Carol Hagan said all they offered you was a reading with Lund. They said they never told you that you had the part."

"But that's not true."

He shrugged. "If it isn't, you're being set up very nicely."

"You believe me, don't you?"

"Why should I?" His face turned somber. The eyes hooded.

"Because we went to bed."

He cocked his head to one side and studied me. "All I know, Diana, is that I called you ten times, and you never returned one call. You're going to have to come down to the Hollywood station tomorrow and give a full statement." He sauntered out of the room to the foyer. I heard the front door open.

"You called twelve times, but who's counting," I yelled after him, and then added. "I was afraid." I heard the door close.

When I went to bed that night I didn't take my sleeping pill. The TV was on. A black-and-white B-movie, starring Bonita Granville and one of those vague male actors that never made it, filled the deadly silence of my room. I thought of Emma looking for her self-worth. How the business and her own conflicted needs had stripped it away from her. But why kill her? She was no threat to Lund or Val or Carol. Carol the Wife. I remembered her at Saks fighting back tears and anger at Lund for not coming home. One mistress she could handle. But two? Did Emma upset the balance?

I lay back on my pillows and closed my eyes. I reached over and felt the cold empty side of the bed. When was I going to stop being afraid to fill this other side? And then I thought of how to find the murderer and call Leo Heath back at the same time. Wrapping my husband's silk paisley robe around me, I went to the kitchen and got my Filofax. I called Carol Hagan. She answered on the fifth ring.

"This is Diana and I know who killed Emma." Then I hung up and called Val and said the exact same thing.

Then I called Leo on his cell phone. A woman answered.

"Is Leo Heath there?"

"Just a sec."

I waited, and then his sleepy voice came on the line. "Yeah?"

"This is Diana. Who's the woman?"

"Let me take a look. Don't know her name."

I told him what I had done.

"You have a death wish?" he growled.

"No. I just don't want to be framed for murder."

"Jesus Christ. I'm coming over. Wait. Are you calling me back or trying to solve a murder?"

"I'm trying to save myself." I hung up. He has a woman in his bed and he doesn't know her name. What the hell was I doing?

I had left the front door unlocked. And now I sat in the living room in the dark, grasping one of Colin's Oscars. It was the only weapon I could think of other than a knife. I just couldn't see myself plunging a blade into Carol Hagan's Prada-clad body. I was coming to the conclusion that maybe I did have a death wish.

Suddenly there was a loud banging on the sliding glass doors. I dropped to the floor and peered around the sofa. Outside Ryan swayed drunkenly, waving a bottle. I let out a sigh and turned the lamp on and then pulled the door open. Before I could tell him to go home and sleep it off, he pushed past me and collapsed on the sofa.

"How could you, Diana? A cop. A gumshoe, a flatfoot dick."

"He wrote a book,"I responded ineptly.

"Was it made into a movie?"

"Yes. But he hasn't written another one. Writer's block. Could we talk about this another time. I'm ..."

"Jesus, a cop who's a writer. How cliché is that? How cliché is writer's block? How could you do that to Colin. He was a real writer."

"Stop it, Ryan."

"If you were going to give his Oscars away, why didn't you give them to me? You know I've always coveted them. Been jealous of them. You know I feel like a meaningless hack compared to him. Successful but meaningless."

"He's dead, Ryan. Go home. "

He took a hit of Tequila from a bottle with a portrait of Frieda Kahlo on the label. Ryan was always looking for the artist outside himself.

He blinked his eyes at me trying to bring me into focus. "Why are you holding that Oscar by its head?"

"I'm solving a murder. And you're in the way."

His lids drooped. "I always wanted an Oscar and you." The bottle fell from his hand as he passed out.

I shook him. He moaned and slapped me away

The door bell rang. I froze. Then I turned the lamp off and squeezed onto the sofa next to Ryan.

"Jesus Christ, it's dark in here." It was Carol Hagan's voice. So it was the wife.

"Diana?" Val's voice. It was the mistress. Did they do everything together including murder? I hadn't thought of that. I turned the light on. They stood in the room, blinking and staring at me.

"What's Ryan Johns doing here?" Val asked.

"He stumbled in and passed out."

"I don't know how anybody can be so successful and such a failure at the same time," Carol remarked.

"Does his presence make things a little awkward?" I asked

"We just want to talk," Carol said

"We don't want to talk, Carol," Val corrected in an exasperated tone. "We're not taking a meeting. We're not doing lunch. I told you not to come with me."

"I had to. After what you did for me." Tears of gratitude ran down her cheeks.

"What did you do for her, Val?" I asked.

"I thought you knew. I killed Emma."

"Actually I thought Carol did it."

"She's a killer but only in business." She pulled a gun from the jacket of her Charles Chang Lima suit.

"The police are on their way," I said.

"I doubt that. Why would they come rushing out in the middle of the night on an actress' whim?"

"How could you kill Emma? She didn't mean anything to Lund," I said.

"Yes, she did." Carol dabbed at her tears with a Hermes scarf.

"But Lund wasn't going to leave you for Emma."

"If he left anybody, it would've been Val. I couldn't have that."

"She was breaking up our family," Val said.

"Family?" I repeated the word as if none of us knew the meaning of it. Maybe we didn't.

"That's how I think of us." Val smiled at Carol.

"I could never be friends with Emma," Carol sniffed. "Not the way I am with Val. She's like the sister I never had."

"There are all kinds of families. We create them however we can. But that's what we *are*." Val spoke philosophically.

Unexpectedly Ryan Johns rose to his feet belching and singing the Sly Stone song, "We Are Family". Startled Val shot at him. He lurched forward and threw up all over her.

Screaming and recoiling Val dropped the gun. I grabbed it. There was a loud banging then the sound of the front door being slammed back against the foyer wall.

Leo Heath ran into the room with his gun drawn. Val fell to her knees. Carol tried to wipe the puke off her with her scarf.

Ryan slumped back onto the sofa. "I've been shot."

"She missed you." I stared at the shattered mirror on the wall.

"What the hell happened?" Leo wrinkled his nose at Val.

"The tequila went with the gun," I said.

Three hours later Ryan was back in his house tucked into his bed. Val and Carol were arrested. I was in my kitchen holding a hot cup of coffee.

Hands in his pockets, Leo leaned the doorway. "I have to get back to the station."

"I want to say something before you leave. I've been thinking about self-worth. Emma's, Val's, Ryan's, and mine. My self-worth isn't so low that I want a man who can't remember the name of the woman he's in bed with."

"She was my sister."

"You were in bed with your sister?"

He grinned. "No, she's staying with me until her house is finished being painted. She happened to answer my cell."

"Oh."

He studied his shoes for a moment, then he studied me. "So were you calling me back?"

"Yes."

"Good."

Two days later my agent informed me that the movie had been canceled. Then the Herbal Heart people called and said I'd gotten the part, but because of the publicity surrounding Emma Parker's death , the arrests of Val Franz and Carol Hagan, and my involvement in it all, they decided to go with a 'lesser known' actress.

I went out and stood on my dilapidated balcony. It took me a moment to realize that the beach was swarming with paparazzi. Their cameras were aimed up at me like the guns of snipers.

"Smile, Diana," they demanded.

I went back inside.

Having acted with child actors, I've always wondered what happens to them. One little girl rattled off her very long résumé to me on the set one day. She was maybe seven or eight and as driven as a diva. What possible future could she have? I saw Tatum O'Neil, who was in the movie Paper Moon, *at a party; she was maybe twelve at the time, standing alone, her head tilting up toward the adults who were ignoring her. Her isolation was palpable. The image stayed with me. I wanted to write about a child star but I could never figure out how to make it a mystery story. Then one day I put Diana Poole at an expensive luncheon supporting Planned Parenthood where a waiter tells her that her daughter wants to see her. Except Diana Poole doesn't have a daughter. Now I had my suspense. The story is about how Hollywood eats its young; and how a desperate girl, who was once a child actor, is determined to have a mother, real or not.*

A HOLLYWOOD ENDING

"Your daughter is waiting for you in the lobby, ma'am." The banquet waiter hovered over me, balancing a tray of coffee pots and cups.

I was sitting at table of ten women at a Planned Parenthood luncheon being held in the banquet room of the Beverly Wilshire Hotel. The women were movie producers, production executives, a director, and an agent. Enormous crystal chandeliers draped from the ceiling splattering their prismatic patterns of light on us like stardust.

"I don't have a daughter," I told him.

"She pointed you out." He moved off to serve the next table.

"Did he say your daughter, Diana?" Beth Dawson sat next to me. She was a producer who had hired me for a small part in her last movie.

"He made a mistake. We're in a ballroom filled with women."

We looked around at the well-dressed, high-powered females. It was a typical Hollywood fundraiser – two million dollars in veneered teeth, three million in face-lifts, four million in pumped-up breasts and puffed-up lips. The rest, as they say, "Priceless."

"I always seem be surrounded by women," Beth said dryly, adjusting the collar of her pink spring jacket.

As with all the things I do now, I was here because it might be good for my career. My husband Colin, a screenwriter, had died suddenly of a heart attack over a year ago. He left me with what the realtors euphemistically call a "tear- down" in Malibu, an old Jaguar, two Oscars – each for Best Screenplay – an empty bank account, and an emptier heart. So I had gone back to what I had been doing before I married him – acting. Except now I was older and the parts were fewer.

I stared at the voluptuous flower arrangement, tuning out the female lawyer who was droning on at the podium, and reflected on how most of us at our table were premenopausal, menopausal, and post menopausal. And how nature had its own prepared plans for us. Sighing, I brushed napkin-lint from my pencil-slim black skirt and fiddled with the cuffs of my white silk blouse. Then I found myself peering back at the row of large double-doors that led to the lobby. I realized I was looking for a girl searching for her mother.

Two hours later I was outside the hotel waiting for my old Jag as the luncheon women scurried into their sleek cars, the high-powered engines purring.

"Are you Diana Poole?" the hotel doorman asked, approaching.

"Yes."

"Your daughter described you perfectly. She said to tell you she couldn't wait. She'd meet you at home."

"My *daughter* gave you my name and described me?"

He nodded. "To a T."

"What did she look like?"

"Your daughter?" he frowned, taken aback by my question. "Blonde."

"How old?"

"You don't know?"

"No, I don't. Tell me."

"Hard to tell. Twenties? You don't look old enough to have a daughter that age."

"That would be an even better complement if I did have a daughter that age."

He looked completely bewildered. I didn't blame him.

Driving back to Malibu, I opened the windows and the sunroof because I couldn't get the Jag's heater to turn off. Sweat ran down the inside of my legs. The wind pulled at my determinedly blonde hair. I kept thinking about the waiter telling me about my daughter. I'd dismissed him by thinking he'd got the wrong woman. But now the conversation with the hotel doorman unnerved me. My daughter was going to meet me at home? *My home? My daughter?*

I began to wonder what a daughter of mine would look like. She would be a natural blonde as I once had been. Her eyes would be blue like mine, too. While my features were settling into a look of defiant permanence, hers would be full of anticipation and discovery. Another loss as breathtaking as my husband's death washed over me. I'd never had a child. Career first. Then Colin's career. Stop it, Diana. I go to a Planned Parenthood luncheon and end up with a phantom daughter. I tried to smile at the irony of the situation, but the sweat on my legs had turned cold.

I checked the rearview mirror to see if a young woman in search of her mother was following me home.

My house, wedged between Pacific Coast Highway and the ocean, was a one story wood and stucco left over from the sixties. Unlocking the front door, I stepped into the tiled foyer and stopped. Listening. The house was just as quiet as it always was when I returned home nowadays. What was I expecting? Still, I felt wary as I walked into the living room. The shabby- but-not-chic furniture, Colin's two Oscars on the fireplace mantle, and the water stain on the ceiling looked exactly as they should. Nothing disturbed.

I went into the kitchen and turned on the small TV, a habit I'd developed to wipe away the isolating silence. A twenty-four hour cable news station broke the quiet. Two sexy pretty blondes who looked as if they'd been cloned were talking about how bad everything was. I felt better.

As I put my purse on the breakfast table, I noticed the knife drawer was open. Had I left it open? I peered into it. Were they all there? How would I know? Colin had been a great cook. The only knife I used was to open take-out cartons. I wasn't sure what utensils I had or didn't have. I slammed the drawer shut. Get a grip, Diana.

I went into the bedroom to kick off my high heels and get out of my too tight skirt. I stopped dead. The bed was perfectly made. I knew I hadn't made it this morning. As usual I'd been running late. Or did I make it? I couldn't remember what I'd done or hadn't done. Inconsistency had become consistent in my life since Colin's death. Then I felt my body tense with an animal-like alertness and I knew there was another person in the room. I whirled around.

A young woman, in early twenties, leaned casually against the jamb of the bathroom doorway. Her hair was bleached blonde. Her sharp intelligent eyes were an appealing gray-blue. They matched the color of her sweater. Low riding jeans revealed a flat muscular midriff. She held her hands behind her back.

"I made the bed for you," she said, smiling. Perfect white teeth.

"Thank you," I said stupidly.

"You should get your security alarm fixed."

"Can't afford to." My heart was racing now. "What are you doing in my house?"

Ignoring the question, she took her hands from behind her back. She held a gun. I took a step back. She pointed the weapon at me, as if were the most natural thing to do under the circumstances.

"You shouldn't leave your bedroom window open. Anybody could break in. You don't remember me, do you?"

"No, I'm sorry..."

I tried to swallow back my fear.

"Don't be. I played your daughter on *Mommy and Me*."

My mind raced backwards, and I vaguely remembered a little girl with hair tinted the color of mine so we would look like a mother and daughter.

"That was a movie for the Lifetime channel. Terrible script." My voice sounded high pitched and desperate.

"Yes, it was." She laughed charmingly.

"You were about eight years old." I didn't know what else to do but keep her in conversation.

"Yes."

" You've grown-up."

"You can't grow-up in Hollywood. You can only grow old."

"You have a point."

She grinned warmly. Freckles dotted the bridge of her up-turned nose. She had the sweet oval face of the girl-next-door. But with the gun and the bad bleach job she looked like a young woman in a Norman Rockwell illustration gone horribly wrong.

"What do you want?" My lips quivered.

"A cup of coffee." She nodded toward the hallway.

I didn't move. I was afraid to walk in front of her. Afraid to turn my back on her.

"I won't stay long. I just want to talk,"

"About what?"

"Acting."

"You want the name of my agent? A recommendation?"

"You think I'm here to network?" she asked, sardonically. "I just want to talk to you. Come on, let's go in the kitchen."

My knees felt weak as I crossed in front of her and walked down the hallway. I could feel her behind me. My shoulder blades pressed inward in anticipation of a bullet. In the living room, I furtively looked out the sliding glass doors hoping to see my neighbor Ryan Johns. He was usually on my deck, interrupting my life, wanting to be let in. But of course not today. There was only the sun, the glittering Pacific Ocean, and my rotting wood balcony.

She sat at my old pine breakfast table still aiming the gun at me.

"Would you mind turning off the news?" she asked. "It's depressing."

I hit the remote. "I'll have to make the coffee."

"Go on."

"Decaf?"

"Caffeine."

With trembling hands, I began to measure and pour in the water. I considered each appliance a possible weapon against her. I took two mugs from the cupboard and put them on the table. These simple tasks helped focus my mind.

"Milk? Sugar?" I asked, politely.

"Both, please."

I set a carton of milk and a small bowl filled with packets on the table. "I don't have real sugar. I use sweeteners."

"They're not good for you."

"I know. But it's so difficult to stay ..."

"Thin?"

"Thin."

"I've struggled with weight my whole life."

"It doesn't show. You look great."

"The last thing I want from you is an inane compliment, Diana. Do you know why I struggled with my weight?"

"No." Facing her, I leaned against the counter near the Mr. Coffee machine which was now gurgling, burping, and brewing.

"Ever since I played your daughter I wanted to look like you. But I ended up looking like my mother."

"Don't we all?" I forced a smile.

The aroma of coffee permeated the kitchen giving it a homey warm atmosphere, and I made a decision. When the carafe was full I would grab it and swing it at her. The shock of the hot liquid scalding her skin would give me a chance to escape. Maybe even try for the gun.

"Were you the one asking for me at the hotel this afternoon?"

"Yes." She tilted her head to one side, studying me. The light from the kitchen window shone hard on her face revealing fine lines around her pretty mouth and tired eyes. She looked exhausted. "Why did you stop acting?"

"I got married."

"So do a lot of actresses, that doesn't end their careers. You were good. You were on the verge of stardom. Why did you settle for being safe?"

"I wouldn't call marriage safe." Mr, Coffee was almost up to the ten cup line.

"I think you were afraid of success." She yawned. "Sorry, it's been a long night and day."

"The caffeine will help." I watched the last few drops drip into the pot.

My heart was in my throat. I casually turned and like any good host, good mother, I retrieved the pot from the burner. Then I spun back toward her. Leaping to her feet she darted backwards out of my reach. Arms extended, she held the gun steady with both hands, like a cop in a TV series.

"I thought you might want to throw that in my face."

My arms were extended too, but I only held a coffee pot in my two hands. "Wouldn't you in my situation?"

"Yes. It's called empathy"

"You're right. All the good actors have it."

"So we're at a stand off. I guess we'll have to carry on our conversation from here. Me holding my gun and you holding your coffee pot. Except your coffee is eventually going to cool, and then you won't have a weapon, and we won't be able to drink it either."

Surprising myself, I slammed the carafe on the table. Coffee slopped. "Sit down and have your damn coffee. And I don't want to be analyzed by someone holding a gun on me. For your information I wasn't afraid of success."

"You sit first. Go."

I sat and took a paper napkin from the pile already on the table and began to wipe up the spilled liquid. It was lukewarm. Even Mr. Coffee was breaking down on me.

She slowly sat down across from me. Her weapon pointed at my chest.

"Were you acting just then when you banged the pot on the table?" she asked

` "I don't know when I'm acting, and when I'm not anymore." With trembling fingers, I rubbed my forehead and pushed my hair back from my face.

"It's the same with me. The more you tap into your own emotions to create a character, a role, the farther away you get from those very emotions that were yours to begin with. May I have some coffee, please?"

I filled the mugs and slid one in her direction. "What's you name? I don't remember it."

"Crystal," she said wistfully. "My mother named me after the character in the TV series *Dynasty*. Mother had dreams. It was her favorite show. I grew up watching all her old VHS tapes of it. We watched them over and over."

"They must be out on DVDs now."

"She won't need them. I hated the show. It was so unreal."

I watched her take a long greedy gulp of coffee. Her hands trembled, too. The gun twitched. But her pinched, strained expression relaxed. Her eyebrows were the color of her freckles, a reddish brown. I assumed her hair must be the same shade. For a moment I glimpsed the innocent young woman with her entire life in front of her. The girl I had imagined in the car driving home. Her eyes met mine. She smiled. Then her expression hardened, and the innocent girl disappeared. The woman who had slipped over the edge returned.

"It seems to me," she said, "if you don't want to be famous you're in the wrong business."

"True. Do you want to be famous?"

"Yes, because I'm a good actress and being good should've brought me fame. But then I grew up, and I couldn't get another decent part."

"It's a cruel business. Sometimes we gain celebrity by ways we don't intend," I said carefully.

"You mean like now? Me breaking into you house? This gun?"

I nodded. "It's the unintended consequences. And I'm sure you don't want that kind of notoriety for doing something ..." I was going to say crazy and thought better of it.

"It's like an improvisation in acting class, isn't it?"

"What is?"

"Us sitting here talking. You trying to figure out what I want. If I'm going to harm you or not."

"And what's your part in this improv?"

"To get to the end."

"What kind of ending do you want?"

"A Hollywood ending."

"Hollywood doesn't have endings to their movies anymore. They just blow things up at the conclusion."

"No narrative, no ending?"

"That's right." She was smart and had wit.

"But I want an old Hollywood ending like when they were writing narratives. Are you a Joan Crawford fan?"

"I loved her in *Mildred Pierce.*"

"That's one of my favorites, too. And she was great in the George Cukor film, *The Women.* She played a woman named Crystal in that movie. I wish my mother had named me after her character."

"But Joan Crawford took Norma Shear's husband away from her in that movie. Maybe your mother didn't think that was appropriate."

"You think my mother had that kind of morality? I told you she watched *Dynasty.* She never saw *The Women.* She hated the old black and white films. How can you be a stage mother and never see the great films?" Tears formed. She wiped them roughly away. "*Daisy Kenyon* was another great Joan Crawford movie."

"That was with Henry Fonda and Dana Andrews." I clutched my coffee mug so tightly my knuckles were white. It was all I had to cling too.

"She had to decide which man to choose. You see, we're having a good conversation, aren't we?" she asked, like a pleading child.

"Yes."

"I could never talk to my mother this way. You know, I think Joan's daughter destroyed her by writing that book."

"You mean *Mommy Dearest*?"

"But I don't blame her. Joan used her daughter as a prop the way my mother did me."

"Is that why you ... ?" I stopped.

"What?"

"Nothing." I had gone too far. I didn't want to know whether she'd done something to her mother. My heart was pounding again.

Her eyes met mine. "You want to know if I killed her, don't you?"

"Look, I'm tired of being scared. Let's keep talking about the old movies. "What are your other Crawford favorites?"

"The one I love the most is *Masquerade.* She was so beautiful in that film."

Shadows grew long across the kitchen floor. The sun was lowering.

"John Garfield played her lover," I said.

"He was a concert violinist in that movie. It's getting dark out."

"What do you want from me?" I blurted, desperately.

"I told you a conversation . Like a mother and daughter who share the same goals."

"I'm not your mother."

"I know that! I'm not crazy." Her body tensed. The gun jerked in her hand. "We're doing an improv. You're my mother. I'm your daughter. You love me instead of just promoting me. You don't resent me because I grew up and couldn't bring in the money anymore. You don't hate me for being an adult. You look scared again."

"I am."

Her voice grew loud and shrill. "I didn't kill her if that's what you're thinking."

I didn't answer.

"I killed my agent."

I sat back in my chair. "You killed your agent?" I didn't know whether to cry or laugh. "Who was he?"

"Ben Black."

"He's my agent. You killed my agent."

"He wasn't right for you."

I put my face in my hands. I was losing it. My pathetic world was turning upside down, and what little I had left to cling to was being taken away by a mad young woman.

"He said some very bad things about you."

I looked at her. "Such as?"

Using her free hand she poured us both more coffee. "He always returns phone calls later in the day when all the assistants and secretaries are gone. Except he never returned mine. So yesterday I was in the outer office. His door was ajar. I could hear him telling a producer that you weren't right for the part of Jillian in the new Josh King movie."

"I just read for that role. They said they wanted to hire me."

"I'm sorry, but he was telling the producer he should sign Pauline Hale instead."

"She can't act her way out of a paper bag."

"He's sleeping with her."

"How do you know?"

"My mother told me. She's also sleeping with him. She discovered them in bed one night."

"Wait a minute. I'm not following all this. Your mother was

sleeping with Ben Black to get you work?"

"No, just because he wanted her."

"And he was also sleeping with that slut Pauline Hale?"

She nodded and glanced quickly out the window. The sun was gone. The light in the kitchen had dimmed. Her expression was wretched, heartbroken.

"Nobody's ever looked out for you, have they?" I said, softly.

"Ben Black told me I was through. He told me that nobody wanted to hire me. It was so Hollywood. My mother told me the same thing. Everyday. Nobody wants me."

Without thinking, I placed my hand on her forearm.

"Now you're not afraid of me even though I killed our agent. But if I had killed my mother ..."

I withdrew my hand. "You were acting weren't you? Improv. You're very good. I believed you killed Ben Black."

Her eyes flashed.

"I was at a luncheon filled with people in the business. If you'd murdered Ben Black last night everybody would be talking about it today. But they weren't because you didn't kill him."

It was dark now except for the illumination of the computerize clock on the microwave and a faint reflection of a waning moon at the window.

"You told the waiter and the hotel door man that you were my daughter because you didn't have a mother anymore." I was still afraid to say the word murdered.

"I had to change my hair color so I wouldn't be recognized. I decided on your color. Not a great job, I know. You were the only person that I wanted to see. I came here this morning to be with you. While I was waiting outside to get up my nerve I saw you leave. I followed you to the hotel and the luncheon. Then I came back here and waited for you."

"So you and I could pretend to be mother and daughter."

"Improv," she said, defensively.

"I know a lot about improvisation," I said softly. "I know even more about mourning. You didn't expect to feel the loss of her, did you?"

"No." Her voice was a whisper.

We were two pale shadows sitting at the kitchen table. A strange calming silence fell between us.

Startling me, she abruptly shoved her chair back and stood. I froze. She closed in on me. Leaning down, she rested her head on my shoulder. I still didn't move. Then I felt the flat side of the gun pressing into my back as she hugged me. I put my hand on her cheek.

"I wish you were my mother. Good-bye, Diana

"Where are you going, Crystal?"

"I want you to stay here. I don't want to shoot you." She left the kitchen.

I remained at the table in the darkness. I thought about Hollywood endings. I thought about Joan Crawford. I thought about the great star walking into the ocean and drowning herself at the end of *Masquerade.* I thought about how quiet my house was once again.

I hurried into the living room. The sliding glass door was open. I went out onto the deck. The fresh ocean air wrapped around me with a familiarity that I never wanted to lose. Except for her lone figure standing at the waters edge, and the thin moon above her, the beach was empty. She dropped the gun and waded into the ocean.

"No!" I screamed.

Kicking off my shoes I ran down to the water. She was rising and falling with each white rimmed wave.

"Don't do it!" The damp wind carried away my scream as I dove into the pounding surf. The cold Pacific water cut me to the bone. I tasted salt. When I came up, I saw a large wave take Crystal and roll her out into the vast blackness. Then another one crashed down on me, sucking me under, and flipping me head over heels. I gasped for air as I clawed my way to the surface and struggled back to shore. Shivering, I searched the horizon for her. I glimpsed her head bob up, as slick and as shinny as a seal's in the moonlight, then vanish.

I ran to my kitchen and called 911. Then I leaned against the counter for support. I took a dishtowel and buried my face in it. I began to cry. I cried for Crystal. I cried for the phantom daughter. I cried for the hell of it.

Gathering myself, I picked up the phone and punched in Ben Black's private number.

"Yes!" he barked.

"I knew you weren't dead."

"Who the hell is this?"

"Diana Poole."

"Are you drunk? Listen, I've had a terrible day. The police have been crawling all over the place. A woman I know was murdered. Her daughter, Crystal, is one of my clients. I think she did it. Crystal came to see me yesterday evening. I had to throw her out of the office. Why do they always come to me when they're has-beens?"

"Do you have bad news for me, Ben?"

"What are you, a mind reader? The producers want to go with Pauline Hale. Sorry, Diana. I worked my ass off to get you the part. It was perfect for you."

"I'm a big girl, Ben. I can handle you screwing me over. But you went to bed with Crystal's mother. And didn't do anything for Crystal. She should've shot you instead." I hit the off button. I hate cell phones – you can't slam the receiver down.

I grabbed Colin's old rain jacket from the laundry room and put it on. Then I waited on the beach for the police. The cold water bit at my bare feet. I turned and looked at the houses lining the shore. The only one with a light on was mine.

SOURCES

"Dirty Blonde," *Sisters in Crime 4*, ed. Marilyn Wallace (Berkley, 1991)

"Another Tented Evening," *Ellery Queen's Mystery Magazine*, March 1996

"Killing the Sixties," *Ellery Queen's Mystery Magazine*, June 1999

"Facing Up," *Ellery Queen's Mystery Magazine*, July 2004

"Tiffany Blue," *Ellery Queen's Mystery Magazine*, March 2002

"The Talking Dead," *Ellery Queen's Mystery Magazine*, June 2003

"The Good Daughter," *Ellery Queen's Mystery Magazine*, August 2007

"What's It Worth?," *Ellery Queen's Mystery Magazine*, December 2008

"A Hollywood Ending," *Ellery Queen's Mystery Magazine*, July 2009

Shooting Hollywood by Melodie Johnson Howe, is set in Goudy Old Style and printed on sixty-pound Natures acid-free recycled paper. The design is by Gail Cross. The first edition was printed in two forms: trade softcover, notchbound; and two hundred copies sewn in cloth, signed and numbered by the author. Each of the clothbound copies includes a separate pamphlet, *Acting Tips* by Melodie Johnson Howe.

Shoopting Hollyqwood was printed and bound by Thomson-Shore, Inc., Dexter, Michigan and published in December 2011 by Crippen & Landru Publishers, Inc., Norfolk, Virginia.

CRIPPEN & LANDRU, PUBLISHERS

P. O. Box 9315
Norfolk, VA 23505
info@crippenlandru.com; toll-free 877 622-6656
www.crippenlandru.com

Crippen & Landru publishes first edition short-story collections by important detective and mystery writers. The following books are currently (May 2011) in print; see our website for full details:

REGULAR SERIES

Speak of the Devil by John Dickson Carr. 1994. Trade softcover. $15.00.

Diagnosis: Impossible, The Problems of Dr. Sam Hawthorne by Edward D. Hoch. 1996. Trade softcover, $19.00.

In Kensington Gardens Once by H.R.F. Keating. 1997. Trade softcover, $12.00.

Shoveling Smoke by Margaret Maron. 1997. Trade softcover, $19.00.

The Ripper of Storyville and Other Tales of Ben Snow by Edward D. Hoch. 1997. Trade softcover. $19.00.

Renowned Be Thy Grave by P.M. Carlson. 1998. Trade softcover, $16.00.

Carpenter and Quincannon by Bill Pronzini. 1998. Trade softcover, $16.00.

Famous Blue Raincoat by Ed Gorman. 1999. Signed, unnumbered cloth overrun copies, $30.00. Trade softcover, $17.00.

The Tragedy of Errors and Others by Ellery Queen. 1999. Trade softcover, $20.00.

McCone and Friends by Marcia Muller. 2000. Trade softcover, $19.00.

Challenge the Widow Maker by Clark Howard. 2000. Trade softcover, $16.00.

Fortune's World by Michael Collins. 2000. Trade softcover, $16.00.

Long Live the Dead: Tales from Black Mask by Hugh B. Cave. 2000. Trade softcover, $16.00.

Tales Out of School by Carolyn Wheat. 2000. Trade softcover, $16.00.

Stakeout on Page Street and Other DKA Files by Joe Gores. 2000. Trade softcover, $16.00.

The Celestial Buffet by Susan Dunlap. 2001. Trade softcover, $16.00.

The Old Spies Club and Other Intrigues of Rand by Edward D. Hoch. 2001. Signed, unnumbered cloth overrun copies, $32.00. Trade softcover, $17.00.

Adam and Eve on a Raft by Ron Goulart. 2001. Signed, unnumbered cloth overrun copies, $32.00. Trade softcover, $17.00.

The Reluctant Detective by Michael Z. Lewin. 2001. Signed, numbered clothbound, $42.00. Trade softcover, $17.00.

Nine Sons by Wendy Hornsby. 2002. Trade softcover, $16.00.

The 13 Culprits by Georges Simenon, translated by Peter Schulman. 2002. Trade softcover, $16.00.

The Dark Snow by Brendan DuBois. 2002. Signed, unnumbered cloth overrun copies, $32.00.

Come Into My Parlor: Tales from Detective Fiction Weekly by Hugh B. Cave. 2002. Trade softcover, $17.00.

The Iron Angel and Other Tales of the Gypsy Sleuth by Edward D. Hoch. 2003. Signed, numbered clothbound, $42.00. Trade softcover, $17.00.

Cuddy – Plus One by Jeremiah Healy. 2003. Trade softcover, $18.00.

Problems Solved by Bill Pronzini and Barry N. Malzberg. 2003. Signed, numbered clothbound, $42.00. Trade softcover, $16.00.

A Killing Climate by Eric Wright. 2003. Trade softcover, $17.00.

Lucky Dip by Liza Cody. 2003. Signed, numbered clothbound, $42.00. Trade softcover, $17.00.

Kill the Umpire: The Calls of Ed Gorgon by Jon L. Breen. 2003. Trade softcover, $17.00.

Suitable for Hanging by Margaret Maron. 2004. Trade softcover, $19.00.

Murders and Other Confusions by Kathy Lynn Emerson. 2004. Signed, numbered clothbound, $42.00. Trade softcover, $19.00.

Byline: Mickey Spillane by Mickey Spillane, edited by Lynn Myers and Max Allan Collins. 2004. Trade softcover, $20.00.

The Confessions of Owen Keane by Terence Faherty. 2005. Signed, numbered clothbound, $42.00. Trade softcover, $17.00.

Murder, Ancient and Modern by Edward Marston. 2005. Signed, numbered clothbound, $43.00. Trade softcover, $18.00.

Murder, 'Orrible Murder! by Amy Myers. 2006. Signed, numbered clothbound, $43.00. Trade softcover, $18.00.

The Verdict of Us All: Stories by the Detection Club for H.R.F. Keating, edited by Peter Lovesey. 2006. Numbered clothbound, $43.00. Trade softcover, $20.00.

The Mankiller of Poojeegai and Other Mysteries by Walter Satterthwait. 2007. Signed, numbered clothbound, $43.00. Trade softcover, $17.00.

Quintet: The Cases of Chase and Delacroix by Richard A. Lupoff. 2008. Signed, numbered clothbound, $43.00. Trade softcover, $17.00.

Murder on the Short List by Peter Lovesey. 2008. Signed, numbered clothbound, $43.00. Trade softcover, $17.00.

Thirteen to the Gallows by John Dickson Carr and Val Gielgud. 2008. Numbered clothbound, $43.00. Trade softcover, $20.00.

A Little Intelligence by Robert Silverberg and Randall Garrett. 2008. Signed, numbered clothbound, $42.00. Trade softcover, $16.00.

A Pocketful of Noses: Stories of One Ganelon or Another by James Powell 2009. Signed, numbered clothbound, $42.00. Trade softcover, $17.00.

A Tale About a Tiger by S. J. Rozan. 2009. Signed, numbered clothbound, $43.00. Trade softcover, $17.00.

The Columbo Collection by William Link. 2010. Trade softcover, $18.00.

Valentino: Film Detective by Loren D. Estleman. 2011. Signed, numbered clothbound, $43.00. Trade softcover, $17.00.

Shooting Hollyuwood: The Diana Poole Stories by Melodie Johnson Howe. Signed, numbered clothbound, $43.00. Trade softcover, $17.00.

CRIPPEN & LANDRU LOST CLASSICS

Crippen & Landru is proud to publish a series of *new* short-story collections by great authors who specialized in traditional mysteries. Each book collects stories from crumbling pages of old pulp, digest, and slick magazines, and most of the stories have been "lost" since their first publication. The following books are in print:

The Newtonian Egg and Other Cases of Rolf le Roux by Peter Godfrey, introduction by Ronald Godfrey. 2002. Trade softcover, $15.00.

Murder, Mystery and Malone by Craig Rice, edited by Jeffrey A. Marks. 2002. Trade softcover, $19.00.

The Sleuth of Baghdad: The Inspector Chafik Stories, by Charles B. Child. Cloth, $27.00. 2002. Trade softcover, $17.00.

Hildegarde Withers: Uncollected Riddles by Stuart Palmer, introduction by Mrs. Stuart Palmer. 2002. Trade softcover, $19.00.

The Spotted Cat and Other Mysteries from the Casebook of Inspector Cockrill by Christianna Brand, edited by Tony Medawar. 2002. Cloth, $29.00. Trade softcover, $19.00.

Marksman and Other Stories by William Campbell Gault, edited by Bill Pronzini; afterword by Shelley Gault. 2003. Trade softcover, $19.00.

Karmesin: The World's Greatest Criminal – Or Most Outrageous Liar by Gerald Kersh, edited by Paul Duncan. 2003. Cloth, $27.00.

The Complete Curious Mr. Tarrant by C. Daly King, introduction by Edward D. Hoch. Cloth, $29.00. 2003. Trade softcover, $19.00.

The Pleasant Assassin and Other Cases of Dr. Basil Willing by Helen McCloy, introduction by B.A. Pike. 2003. Cloth, $27.00. Trade softcover, $18.00.

Murder – All Kinds by William L. DeAndrea, introduction by Jane Haddam. 2003. Cloth, $29.00. Trade softcover, $19.00.

The Avenging Chance and Other Mysteries from Roger Sheringham's Casebook by Anthony Berkeley, edited by Tony Medawar and Arthur Robinson. 2004. Cloth, $29.00. Trade softcover, $19.00.

Banner Deadlines: The Impossible Files of Senator Brooks U. Banner by Joseph Commings, edited by Robert Adey; memoir by Edward D. Hoch. 2004. Cloth, $29.00.

The Danger Zone and Other Stories by Erle Stanley Gardner, edited by Bill Pronzini. 2004. Trade softcover, $19.00.

Dr. Poggioli: Criminologist by T.S. Stribling, edited by Arthur Vidro. Cloth, $29.00. 2004. Cloth, $29.00. Trade softcover, $19.00.

The Couple Next Door: Collected Short Mysteries by Margaret Millar, edited by Tom Nolan ·2004 Trade softcover· $19 00

Sleuth's Alchemy: Cases of Mrs. Bradley and Others by Gladys Mitchell, edited by Nicholas Fuller. 2004. Trade softcover, $19.00.

Who Was Guilty? Two Dime Novels by Philip S. Warne/Howard W. Macy, edited by Marlena E. Bremseth. 2004. Cloth, $29.00.

Slot-Machine Kelly by Michael Collins, introduction by Robert J. Randisi. Cloth, $29.00. 2004. Trade softcover, $19.00.

The Evidence of the Sword by Rafael Sabatini, edited by Jesse F. Knight. 2006. Cloth, $29.00. Trade softcover, $19.00.

The Casebook of Sidney Zoom by Erle Stanley Gardner, edited by Bill Pronzini. 2006. Cloth, $29.00. Trade softcover, $19.00.

The Detections of Francis Quarles by Julian Symons, edited by John Cooper; afterword by Kathleen Symons. 2006. Cloth, $29.00. Trade softcover, $19.00.

The Trinity Cat and Other Mysteries by Ellis Peters (Edith Pargeter), edited by Martin Edwards and Sue Feder. 2006. Trade softcover, $19.00.

The Grandfather Rastin Mysteries by Lloyd Biggle, Jr., edited by Kenneth Lloyd Biggle and Donna Biggle Emerson. 2007. Cloth, $29.00. Trade softcover, $19.00.

Masquerade: Ten Crime Stories by Max Brand, edited by William F. Nolan. 2007. Cloth, $29.00. Trade softcover, $19.00.

Dead Yesterday and Other Mysteries by Mignon G. Eberhart, edited by Rick Cypert and Kirby McCauley. 2007. Cloth, $30.00. Trade softcover, $20.00.

The Battles of Jericho by Hugh Pentecost, introduction by S.T. Karnick. 2008. Cloth, $29.00. Trade softcover, $19.00.

The Minerva Club, The Department of Patterns and Other Stories by Victor Canning, edited by John Higgins. 2009. Cloth, $29.00. Trade softcover, $19.00.

The Casebook of Gregory Hood by Anthony Boucher and Denis Green, edited by Joe R. Christopher. 2009 Cloth, $29.00. Trade softcover, $19.00.

Murder at the Stork Club and Other Stories by Vera Caspary, edited by Barbara Emrys. 2009. Cloth, $29.00. Trade softcover, $19.00.

Appleby Talks About Crime by Michael Innes, edited by John Cooper. 2010. Cloth, $28.00. Trade softcover, $18.00.

Ten Thousand Blunt Instruments by Philip Wylie, edited by Bill Pronzini 2010. Cloth, $29.00. Trade softcover, $19.00..

The Exploits of the Patent Leather Kid by Erle Stanley Gardner, edited by Bill Pronzini. 2010. Cloth, $29.00. Trade softcover, $19.00.

The Duel of Shadows by Vincent Cornier, edited by Mike Ashley. 2011. Cloth, $28.00. Trade softcover, $18.00.

SUBSCRIPTIONS

Subscribers agree to purchase each forthcoming publication, either the Regular Series or the Lost Classics or (preferably) both. Collectors can thereby guarantee receiving limited editions, and readers won't miss any favorite stories. Subscribers receive a discount of 20% off the list price (and the same discount on our backlist) and a specially commissioned short story by a major writer in a deluxe edition as a gift at the end of the year.

The point for us is that, since customers don't pick and choose which books they want, we have a guaranteed sale even before the book is published, and that allows us to be more imaginative in choosing short story collections to issue. That's worth the 20% discount for us.